A man wa...
idling car...

Caleb had a split second to decide what to do. By the time he ran around the car, he might not get to Alana before the stranger had her inside his vehicle, and then things could get bad. He turned to the dog. "Go, Rex!"

Rex was off like a shot, straight to the woman he'd liked on sight. The dog leaped at the man dragging Alana, and the three of them dropped to the lawn. The attacker loosened his hold and Alana scrambled away. There was a yelp from Rex as the stranger pushed the dog off.

The man jumped for the car and the vehicle pulled away. Caleb nearly touched the vehicle before it was out of his grasp. He noted the license plate and then turned to Alana and Rex. Alana was pulling herself upright.

"You okay, Alana?"

She nodded. "Good enough."

But something was going on. There was no proof yet that it was connected to the jewelry-store heist all those years ago, but people didn't try to abduct veterinarians in daylight for fun. Who was after her?

Anne Galbraith grew up in the cold in Canada but now lives on a sailboat in the Caribbean, where she writes stories about happy-ever-afters. She enjoys sailing the blue waters, exploring new countries and sharing her characters with anyone who will read them. She's been a daughter, sister, wife, mother, teacher, accountant and is now thrilled to add author to that list.

Books by Anne Galbraith

Love Inspired Suspense

Kidnap Threat

Love Inspired Cold Case

Out of the Ashes

HIDDEN EVIDENCE

ANNE GALBRAITH

LOVE INSPIRED
INSPIRATIONAL ROMANCE

LOVE INSPIRED®
INSPIRATIONAL ROMANCE

Recycling programs
for this product may
not exist in your area.

ISBN-13: 978-1-335-46845-1

Hidden Evidence

For questions and comments about the quality of this book, please contact us at CustomerService@Harlequin.com.

Love Inspired
22 Adelaide St. West, 41st Floor
Toronto, Ontario M5H 4E3, Canada
www.LoveInspired.com

Printed in U.S.A.

And ye shall know the truth,
and the truth shall make you free.
—*John* 8:32

To the animals who don't have a choice, but still serve

Chapter One

The front door was open.

Alana froze in place, door key in her hand. Again?

A week ago, the door had been unlocked when she came home from her veterinary clinic. She thought she'd forgotten to use the key when she left for work, though she'd never done that before. When she entered the house, she'd found some of her things moved around: papers in her office, items in her dresser drawers.

She'd called the police, but not much could be done. Everyone assumed the door had been left unlocked and that some kids, or maybe a passing vagrant, had been looking for cash or things to sell. Nothing was missing. She'd been a little creeped out, looking over her shoulder for the first few days, but had finally shrugged it off.

Now all that worry rushed back with a vengeance. Had the intruder returned? She knew she hadn't left the door unlocked this morning. She'd double-checked every time after the last incident.

The smart thing would be to return to her car, lock herself inside with the engine running and call the police. Except for the voice in her head questioning: *Had* she locked the door? Was there any way the door could have unlatched? If someone were in there, was it someone starving, desperate for just a bit of cash or food to eat? She didn't want to be the boy crying wolf, if she had forgotten. She could peek.

A second voice told her not to risk it, but with a quickly breathed prayer for help, she took a quiet step forward and touched her hand to the door, silently nudging it further ajar.

She blinked at the chaos in front of her. The front door opened to the living room. Couch cushions and pillows were tossed on the floor. She took a couple of steps inside, and saw, through the dining room and into the kitchen, cabinets open, contents spilling everywhere.

Anger coursed through her veins, heating her blood, while fear shot ice down her back. She wanted to find whoever had done this, but she remained frozen in place.

Then she saw movement, and a man in a mask.

For a fraction of a second, they stared at each other, unmoving, before he started toward her.

Alana whipped around, adrenaline lighting up her muscles, urging flight, not fight. But she slipped on the entry mat, several feet out of its normal position, and saw the threshold rushing toward her. Her hands moved to stop the fall, but too slowly, and the ridged metal was the last thing she saw before blackness took over.

"I'm fine, Mr. Conners." Alana smiled at her neighbor, a retired police officer, standing on her porch with a worried expression on his face. "The bruise looks

bad, but the EMTs said I didn't have a concussion."
She gently touched her forehead.

Mr. Conners had been the one to find her, stretched
out in her front hallway. Alana had soon regained consciousness, but he'd insisted on an ambulance before
calling the police. It was past midnight, and Alana
thought Mr. Conners needed to get to bed.

"I'm worried about you. And not just the head." The
man's lips were a firm line, his gaze narrowed on her.

Alana leaned against her front doorframe. The
house had been lit up since the police went through it.
She presumed they'd looked for clues.

Alana hadn't been able to help much. She had a
fuzzy recollection of a man in black with a mask on his
face. From the distance she'd seen him, she wasn't sure
of his height or weight beyond average, but she couldn't
swear that he hadn't been hunched over or wearing
lifts. She shivered at the recollection, vague as it was.

"You can't stay here."

Alana shook her head. "I'm not going to. The house
is a disaster." Nothing had been put back in order, and
fingerprint powder coated the place. She couldn't think
about cleaning up, since she was already running on
fumes as far as energy went.

"I'm just going to grab some sheets. I'll stay at the
apartment over the garage until I can get the alarm
installed."

Mr. Conners hadn't needed to talk her into that. She'd
entertained the possibility after the first incident. Now
she'd left a message at the company Mr. Conners recommended so they'd get it first thing in the morning.

"Will you be safe there?"

Alana hoped so. The police had promised a car would

patrol regularly. And she was going to shove something in front of the door. Something heavy, so it couldn't open.

"You should have someone stay with you. I could get Miriam."

Alana shook her head. "Let your wife sleep. If there is some danger, I don't want to risk anyone else. Besides, I'm not alone."

Alana made a praying gesture with her hands.

"Right," Mr. Conners said. "I need to trust as well. I think you should stay in the apartment until you have the alarm installed."

"I agree. It's a good thing we haven't rented it for a while."

After her mother's first stroke, Alana hadn't bothered trying to find another tenant when the student who'd been there moved out. And since her mother's passing six months ago, Alana hadn't been willing to make the effort. It was no longer a *we* who would be renting it out. A wave of grief moved over her. Thank goodness her mother hadn't been in the house today. Normally she'd taken the summers off, which meant the intruders could have found her there.

Alana swallowed the lump in her throat. "I'll get those sheets, and deal with this in the morning."

Mr. Conners nodded. "Miriam is going to call people at the church. We'll get some hands here to help clean up. You should rest."

"I'll gladly take the help, but I'm still going to work. It's the morning I spay and neuter for the animal shelter."

Mr. Conners frowned at her, but she knew it was concern, not anger. "Maybe you should take the day off. Or even the week."

Some of the anger returned. "I don't know who did

this or why, but they're not going to stop me from living my life, and the shelter isn't going to suffer."

Mr. Conners looked around the house. "I want you to message me when you leave for work, and when you're coming home. I'll make sure things are safe for you."

Alana gave him a wavery smile. "I'll take you up on that."

Caleb read the message again, as if another reading would give him more details.

Come to my office.

He couldn't think of anything he'd done wrong, so was this about his transfer? Maybe he was getting into the undercover training course? He picked up a notepad and pen and made his way to the corner office. He knocked, and opened the door when he heard the gruff "Come in."

No one could mistake the man behind the desk for anything but a cop. The short hair and sharp jaw, with a bulky figure still promising a lot of strength despite the broadening waistline. But mostly it was the eyes, keen and always assessing. Yoxall was a lifelong RCMP officer, and he was one of the best. Now he had a desk job, but Caleb had heard the stories. He respected the man and hoped to be just like him.

"Have a seat, Drekker."

Caleb did so, trying to read the man's face to get a hint at what was coming.

"Something's come up."

Yoxall's desk was chronically neat. He had one notepad in front of him, with scribbles on it that would be impossible to read even if the paper weren't upside down. Caleb shifted in his chair and waited. Patience was a virtue that Yoxall respected.

"I know you want to go undercover. I'm working on making that happen. In the meantime, I have an unofficial chance for you, but I'll warn you up front—it's a babysitting job."

For a moment, Caleb took that literally and wanted to protest that he didn't have experience with small children.

"Twenty-five years ago, a woman and her daughter went into our witness protection program. The mother died in January. The daughter is still there, still with the new identity. But in the past week her place was broken into twice. She was injured the second time."

Caleb's mouth opened to ask questions, but Yoxall put his hand up.

"Almost everyone involved directly in the case has died in the last twenty-five years. The daughter was only four when she was relocated, so there's no reason to suspect anything from the past is part of this.

"But."

There was something in the *but*, something that lent uneasiness to the conversation.

"I want you to go to Winnipeg."

"Winnipeg?" Caleb didn't mean to interrupt, but honestly, Winnipeg?

Yoxall raised his brows. "You know where Winnipeg is, Drekker?"

Caleb nodded.

"It's the start of the prairies and it's cold and windy in winter, but you're lucky this is summer and instead you get hot and dry."

"Yes, sir."

Yoxall narrowed his eyes. "The woman's neighbor, a retired cop, was their contact. He's the one who called me. He has asked the daughter if his friend's son can stay in the garage apartment on her property. This son is supposedly writing a book. Think of something you can study up on that relates to Winnipeg to maintain a cover. Then just keep an eye out in case someone wants something from her, especially if it connects to this old case."

Caleb fought to keep his body still. Sure, this was babysitting, like Yoxall said, with a good chance of nothing interesting happening, but it was a start. A chance to see if he could do it, put on another persona and inhabit it well enough that people believed in his cover. And if he succeeded with this, maybe it would help get him to the top of the list for the undercover program?

But maybe not if it were unofficial. Could he ask why? Did he want to, if this were an opportunity he might never get again?

"When would I start?"

"I'd like to have you on a plane tomorrow, but you need time to wrap up what you're currently doing and work on a cover. Three days?"

"Absolutely." There were still questions in his mind about the unofficial part. Was there really a problem in Winnipeg, or was this all set up as a test for him?

"You can't tell anyone here what you're doing." That caught Caleb's wandering attention.

"Why is that, sir?"

Yoxall leaned back. "Has your father ever mentioned Walter Abbott to you?"

Caleb ran the name through his mental filing cabinet. "I don't believe so. Is he in the undercover program?"

Yoxall snorted. "No. He's dead. He's one of the players in what happened twenty-five years ago. I'm going to tell you a story, and it remains with you. As far as everyone knows, you're on leave."

Caleb frowned. "My family?"

"Talk to your dad. He can give you more of the background on this. It might help. It's why I thought of you first when I got the call from Winnipeg."

Caleb had a lot of questions for his father now. "The story? Sir?"

Yoxall tapped his fingers on the notepad. "Twenty-five years ago, an off-duty City of Toronto police officer was killed in a jewelry store. Walter Abbott. He was your father's best friend."

How did Caleb not know this?

"The jewelry store owner, Greg Campbell, was fencing stolen goods. He went to prison for that, and for manslaughter in the death of the cop. Campbell's wife and daughter went into WP after she testified against him, and he died in prison about ten years ago."

"The daughter is who you want me to babysit."

Yoxall nodded. "What was kept quiet was that Walter Abbott was blackmailing Campbell to set up a fake robbery."

"He was dirty?"

Yoxall nodded. "It was difficult for your father. They'd gone through training together, and were partners, until your dad transferred to the RCMP, where I met him. Your dad was a good cop, and it was a shame what happened to him."

The OPP, Ontario Provincial Police, had jurisdiction in the province of Ontario, and the RCMP covered federal issues there. Most of the Canadian provinces used the RCMP for their policing, but Ontario and Quebec were populated enough to have their own organizations, and some cities had their own police force. Caleb knew his dad had been with the RCMP for a short period before he started his private security firm, but not that he'd been with the city police as well.

"It was a sordid story that would end there, except…"

Right. There had to be more, if they were still worried about the daughter.

"There was good reason to think Abbott wasn't working alone. Campbell swore no one else was in the store when Abbott died. He said the cop had startled him, and he'd shot at him with the pistol he kept for protection. The guy fell and hit the corner of a glass cabinet, which killed him."

Caleb cleared his throat. "Why do you think Campbell was lying?"

"We couldn't find the security tape of that day in the jewelry store. Campbell said he'd forgotten to put a tape in—he was still using videotapes back then. Also, about half the fenced goods for the job that he served time for were missing. They've never shown up, best we know."

"You think someone was working with Campbell, or Abbott?"

"Campbell's wife insisted another cop was involved. If Abbott had an accomplice, and it wasn't your father, who was in hospital, the first suspect would be his partner at the time. Bobby Fowler. Fowler's father headed up WP for the OPP. Fowler had an alibi, but it was suspect as far as I was concerned."

"What happened to the younger Fowler?"

"He got moved around, and I lost track. His father wasn't happy with our suspicions. The OPP weren't involved, and it was only the RCMP who were questioning things, and that was because of your dad. We had no say in what the city police did.

"Now Fowler Senior is retiring from the force, and launching a political campaign."

"So maybe the Fowlers are cleaning up their dirty laundry?"

"Don't get too excited. It might just be a junkie looking for money for a fix. Now I've got one of those endless stupid meetings to get to. I'll put in the paperwork for your leave and give you Conners's contact info—that's the cop in Winnipeg. He was their WP contact until he retired a couple of years ago, and he wasn't replaced. Ask your dad for the rest of the story. I'll give you a number to call if something comes up but avoid any cops other than Conners."

Caleb stood, the dismissal obvious. "I'll do my best to find out if anything is going on and keep her safe."

"One more thing. The daughter is a vet—veterinarian. So we're giving you a dog to get on her good side."

Caleb's jaw dropped. "A dog?"

Chief frowned. "You allergic or something?"

"My mother is. I've never had a dog."

"You have one now."

Caleb threw his shaving bag into his duffel. That was the final item he needed.

He'd spent the last three days creating a cover story.

He was a former army recruit. That should explain if
he gave off a law enforcement vibe or revealed any fa-
miliarity with weapons. His alter ego, Caleb Johnson,
was taking a master's degree in marketing, thanks to
a small legacy from his great-aunt, and he'd come to
Winnipeg to study the PR involved with the loss of
their professional hockey team in the 1990s and its
subsequent return to the city. Caleb was a hockey fan,
so he could talk about the sport knowledgeably, and
it would be a good gateway when he interacted with
people. His cousin had just finished a master's in marketing, so he had a resource if needed.

There was a knock on the door of his town house.
Caleb found his father on the step. They'd had a fare-
well dinner last night at his family's home, just his
mother and father and siblings. They knew roughly
what he was doing, but other than his dad, no one
knew the name, case or even where Caleb was going.

"Hey, Dad. I'm just finishing packing. Can we talk
upstairs?"

His father followed him and stopped in the doorway
of his room. He was dressed in his work clothes: a polo
shirt with the name of the security firm on it, and kha-
kis. He was a tall man, still in good shape, and looked
able to physically handle anyone breaking into one of
the sites the firm protected. He barely limped from
the long-ago injury that had halted his police career.

He stared at Caleb's suitcase for a moment. "The
truth will set you free."

Caleb tilted his head away from the computer bag
he'd been checking. Wary of traffic in the city, Caleb
was leaving the house within the hour. When his father said he'd come talk to Caleb before his flight,

Caleb hadn't expected the talk to start with a verse of Scripture.

"Do you think your friend Abbott was set up?"

His father shook his head. "I talked to Wilma, his wife, after his death. She knew something was going on with him. She found money he shouldn't have had."

"Maybe—"

"No, Caleb. I knew the man. He was kind and likable and would give you the shirt off his back, but he was a follower. He did what he was told, and he didn't think too much about the morals of it. I worried, leaving him when I transferred to the RCMP."

"Why did you transfer, then, and what were you worried about?"

"My dream was to work undercover, and I had a better shot at what I wanted with the Mounties. The only problem was whether Walter would do something stupid. And he did. I was at the trial—Campbell's. The evidence was conclusive. Walter had discovered that the guy was fencing stolen goods, and he didn't turn in the evidence."

"Am I going on a wild-goose chase?"

His father narrowed his eyes and crossed his arms. "No, you're not. I know Walter could never have come up with that idea on his own. Campbell lied—there was someone else involved. I've always thought it was Fowler."

"His partner."

"Fowler came up with an alibi, and his father's connections helped him, but there was no way he could have been ignorant of what Walter was doing."

Caleb zipped up his bag.

"So why did Campbell lie?"

His dad shoved his hands in his pockets. "He had a wife and daughter. If they were threatened, he'd have lied to protect them. After his wife testified, they were hidden away in WitPro, and Campbell took the rap for fencing and manslaughter, but Fowler Senior could have pulled strings, found them."

Caleb pulled his phone off the charger, seeing the notification from the airlines about his flight leaving on time.

"What's happening now? If this is somehow connected."

"Fowler Senior is making a run for office."

"That's what Yoxall said. But Campbell is dead, his wife is dead, and his daughter was just a kid. Why is he worried about something that was taken care of all those years ago?"

"This is speculation, but I think he can't afford to have any dirt dug up, not right now. If there's any evidence that his son committed a crime, and an implication that Fowler covered for him, it puts a big hole in his law-and-order platform."

Caleb leaned against his dresser. "If a security tape exists, like Yoxall suspects, you think Fowler Junior is on it, and the tape shows he was there. Why would Campbell hide it back then if it would prove Fowler Junior was there? He could still have got protection for his family."

"You wouldn't know this, son, but those videotapes were fragile. Run a magnet near one and you could lose everything on it."

Caleb had no idea if it was that easy, but his dad would know better than him. "You think Fowler would have done that, or had someone do it to protect his son?"

"He's an ambitious guy. He may have been planning this foray into politics for a long time, or he may just have been a protective father."

"Would a videotape be usable now, even if someone found it?"

"Maybe. Maybe there are fingerprints that would implicate Fowler Junior. If someone is targeting the daughter, it makes me think there's something out there."

Caleb considered. "If this evidence exists, or existed then, it was hidden. It couldn't still be at the daughter's home, could it?"

"Who knows? It would explain why they broke in. Maybe it was destroyed, or maybe this is nothing."

Caleb straightened. "Let's hope I can convince the daughter to trust me, just in case. And that reminds me, I have to go pick up my partner once I land, and hope he paves the way."

"Partner?" His dad frowned. "I didn't know you had anyone working with you."

"The daughter is a veterinarian, so they're sending me with a retired K-9 dog."

His dad grinned. "Really? But you don't even like dogs."

Caleb shrugged. "I never had a chance to find out, since Mom was allergic."

"Didn't the neighbor's dog bite you once?"

"Yeah. When I was just a kid. But I hardly remember that."

"And your friend's dog always ran away from you. Couldn't stand to be close to you."

Caleb waved the memory away. "The dog was afraid of almost everyone."

"Well, this one won't be afraid of you."

Caleb ignored the twist in his stomach. "We're both professionals. His handler will be a short drive away, so I just have to take the dog for some walks or something. It will be fine."

His dad slapped his shoulder. "Good luck. I'm proud of you, carrying on the family tradition. I always wanted to work undercover like my father did. It's dangerous, but it's the only way to get some of the scum out there. We'll be praying for you."

"Thanks, Dad. I appreciate it. I'll be in touch."

"Remember—don't be afraid of the truth. Pursue it and find out what really happened with Walter."

Chapter Two

Alana had carefully scheduled her day so that she could be at the house when her new tenant arrived. She wanted to meet him as soon as possible. It was a good thing that she trusted Mr. Conners, because she was having second thoughts about having a stranger around.

She was living in the house, with the alarm installed, but since the second break-in, Alana found herself looking over her shoulder, at home, walking the streets, or going to her car after work. It wasn't logical. Because whoever had broken into her house wasn't interested in her; they'd come for just her things, and there was no reason to think they'd be waiting for her when she left work.

She prayed, finding comfort in that, and in the familiar. Her routines, her neighbors, her coworkers. What if another new face upset her? But she'd told Mr. Conners his friend could stay.

The man had been in the army, Mr. Conners said, and was now taking a marketing degree and wanted to do research about how Winnipeg had lost and regained its hockey team for a book. He was single, about thirty, and Alana had glared at Mr. Conners to warn him against any matchmaking.

The new tenant, Caleb Johnson, had asked Mr. Conners about local churches, so he should be a man of faith. And he'd made sure she would welcome a dog. All that sounded good, but he was still a stranger, and she needed to see for herself.

Of course, the day she wanted to leave work early was the day an emergency popped up. Instead of getting home, with time to shower and prepare to meet her new tenant, she ended up rushing from work just to make it on time for his expected arrival. She pulled into her driveway and found an SUV parked in front of her side of the garage, hatch open. It made her more irritable. She frowned at the back of the man standing behind his vehicle.

She pulled to a stop on the wrong side of the drive and opened her door, determined to recapture some of her poise.

"Hello, Mr. Johnson." She did her best to keep all annoyance out of her voice.

He swiveled to face her. His hair was dark and he had deep brown eyes, with pale, slightly freckled skin. Straight nose, generous mouth, holding himself rigidly upright. She had to look up at him, since he stood over six feet tall, and was well-built. He looked capable of protecting someone. Or hurting them. She stepped back.

"Uh, hi. Are you Alana Travers?"

"I am. Sorry, I meant to be here to welcome you, but something came up at the clinic. If you want to follow me up the stairs—"

Johnson turned to the SUV again. "Sure, just let

me…" He stared into the back of his vehicle, looking even more tense.

What did he have back there?

Alana stepped over to get a look. There was a dog crate in the back and, inside, a German shepherd looking out through the bars. She'd said a dog was fine, so why was he worried?

"Feel free to let your dog out. This is a dog-friendly neighborhood, and I had my own dog until she passed a few months ago. What's yours named?"

Johnson didn't move to open the crate. "Rex."

"I'd love to meet Rex."

It sounded like Johnson muttered "Me, too" but that didn't make any sense.

He stretched out a hand to the crate. Rex stood, ready to be free. Alana wondered how long the pair had been traveling.

Then the man dropped his hand again. He shoved it through his hair. "He doesn't have a leash on. If I open the door, is he going to burst out and run away?"

Alana frowned. Didn't the man know his own dog? "Does he often run away?"

"No?"

Alana didn't know why the man couldn't handle this, but the dog didn't deserve to suffer. If the guy couldn't let the dog out of the crate without all this dithering, who knew if the animal had water, and how long it had been in there?

"Give me the leash." She moved forward, crowding the man, and he stepped back. He pointed to a leash on the roof of the crate. At least it was a good quality one, showing some wear.

"Sit," Alana told Rex. He sat, waiting patiently. She

grabbed the leash, snap ready to go, and flicked the crate open with one hand while she stood in front of him. The dog was large enough to have knocked her over, but she hoped the visual blocking would keep him in place.

The dog stayed seated.

Alana held out a hand, and the dog sniffed. No sign of aggression. She moved slowly, snapping the lead onto the collar. Then she stood back, the dog still waiting.

"Down."

The dog promptly jumped from the vehicle and stood still.

Alana turned. "He doesn't appear to want to make a break for it."

Mr. Johnson's face was flushed, and Alana didn't want to admit that it made him even more attractive. She held out the leash.

"He probably needs to relieve himself. He's welcome to any of the trees."

"Thank you, Ms. Travers."

"Alana is fine. Especially if we're going to be neighbors."

"Then I'm Caleb." He held out his hand to her. Alana shook, noting that his seemed large and capable. Even if curiously reluctant to come close to his own animal.

"Do you want to take Rex to stretch his legs for a few minutes? I'll get the keys to the apartment."

Caleb's feet shifted. He turned to Rex. Rex was waiting patiently but paying more attention to Alana than his owner.

Caleb flicked the leash. "Let's go, Rex."

Rex looked at him, still waiting. Caleb took a step, and Rex followed. Caleb's gaze flickered to the dog, then Alana, then the closest tree.

"Is there a problem?" She didn't want to interfere, but the man was so uncomfortable with the animal that she had to wonder what the story was.

"Um… I just got Rex. His owner, my great-uncle, died a couple of weeks ago. One of the reasons I wanted to come out to Winnipeg was so I could pick Rex up and get to know him. I've never had a dog before."

Alana blinked. That explained the awkwardness.

"Would you like me to show you how to walk him?"

Caleb smiled, relieved, and Alana couldn't resist responding. "Please. I'd be grateful. My mother is allergic, so we've never had pets. At least, none with fur. And I know it's stupid, but I'm afraid I'm going to do something wrong, and he'll run away or bite or something."

Rex was responding to Caleb's body language and smell, and the animal couldn't relax if Caleb didn't. So far, Rex showed every indication of being well trained and was behaving beautifully. Surely, if she just helped them get acquainted, they'd be fine.

She couldn't resist helping someone with their animal. And if they were going to be living next door, she'd be helping them and herself.

All her frustration from work and the drive home was gone. She wasn't worried about having a stranger around. She had a feeling that having Caleb and Rex nearby was going to be good.

Caleb had worried that he'd messed up this assignment before it started, with the problems he was having with Rex. For a while, Caleb wasn't sure he'd even arrive at Alana's with the dog.

The man who had assumed the care of Rex after Rex

retired was himself a retired K-9 cop. But the day before Caleb's flight landed in Winnipeg, he'd had a heart attack. Rex had been left with a neighbor while the man's wife attended him in hospital. Caleb hadn't had a chance to learn how to handle Rex from his trainer. The neighbor had been distracted, worried about the man in hospital. He'd been told that Rex was a great dog and responded to most people well, and was given the dog's supplies.

Caleb was not most people when it came to dogs. Alana would think he was useless, someone who needed rescuing. In that case, she wouldn't trust him to help her. But things were working out. He was interacting with Alana more than he'd expected at their first meeting.

Alana took Rex's lead and showed Caleb how to hold it. She said, "Heel," and Rex walked at her side, the leash slack between them. When she stopped, Rex did as well, and sat.

"Your great-uncle must have trained him well."

Caleb nodded. It wasn't his great-uncle, it was the K-9 unit trainers in Winnipeg, but he couldn't tell Alana that. They didn't want any connection to the police or an undercover operation to come out.

Caleb was undercover, and lying by omission and commission was part of the job. It still felt wrong, though. He didn't want to deceive Alana, but if he was going to be an agent, carry on the legacy of his grandfather, he had to get used to it. He just hadn't expected it to be so difficult. Alana wasn't a criminal. Yoxall had checked her out thoroughly and found nothing suspicious. Her neighbor, the former WP contact Conners, had been there almost every day of her life. If anyone was clean, it was Alana.

Alana explained that body language was important with animals and coached him as he took over the
leash. Her chestnut brown hair was pulled back in a
ponytail, and her coffee-colored eyes were intent. Rex
gave him a look, one that Caleb was sure expressed
the dog's lack of confidence in Caleb's abilities, but his
training was good, and Rex did as asked.

They returned to Alana's house, Caleb holding the
leash, but Rex walking closer to Alana than to Caleb.
Maybe he just wasn't a dog person.

"Give me a moment to grab the keys for the garage
apartment."

"Not a problem." A tug on the leash, and Caleb
brought Rex over to the side of the car.

"Stay?" He watched Rex to see if this was one of
the commands Rex would obey. The dog sat, eyes on
Caleb.

Okay, then. Caleb opened the door to the rear seat.
He had a couple of duffel bags there with his clothes
and another one with Rex's gear. As well as a large bag
of dog food. Caleb had noted the brief feeding instructions on his phone.

He reached for the dog food, one eye on Rex. Rex
was still sitting in place, though his attention was on
the street. Caleb heard a car but couldn't imagine that
was what had caught the dog's attention. Cars drove by
regularly, even if slowly. Maybe a girl dog was walking by, and Rex was a flirt. As long as Rex stayed put,
he could ogle as many other dogs as he chose.

Caleb grabbed the bag, extra large for his large pet,
biceps straining. The dog must eat a ton. He tugged
the bag of food off the seat and twisted to drop it on
the ground beside him. He heard the bang of a screen

door, so Alana must have the keys. Good. A couple of trips up the stairs and he'd be settled in.

A scream, suddenly cut off. Rex was almost levitating in his sit position. Caleb looked over the SUV's roof and saw a man, unknown to him, with his arms wrapped around Alana. One hand covered her mouth and he was dragging her toward the car idling on the street in front of the house.

He had a split second to decide what to do. His gun was in a lockbox in his luggage since his cover had no reason to be carrying it on his person. He was just supposed to babysit. Yoxall and Conners had thought there might be another break-in, not an abduction.

By the time he ran around the car he might not get to Alana before the stranger had her inside his vehicle, and then things could get bad. He turned to the dog. "Go, Rex!"

He wasn't sure what the attack command was, but once Rex was released from the stay Caleb had given him, he was off like a shot, straight to the woman he'd liked on sight.

Caleb pushed himself to follow as quickly as possible. Rex leaped at the man dragging Alana, now close to the idling car, and the dog and the two people dropped to the lawn. The attacker loosened his hold and Alana scrambled away. There was a shot from someone in the car, and a yelp from Rex as the stranger pushed the dog off.

For a moment the man paused, eyes flickering to Alana, who was still too close, and then to Caleb, who was now almost on him. He jumped for the car, the vehicle pulling away as he did so. Caleb nearly touched the car before it was out of his grasp. He noted the license plate, and then turned to Alana and Rex.

Alana was pulling herself upright. Caleb took a step in her direction, worried about her well-being, but her attention was on the dog.

"Rex!"

Caleb followed her gaze and noted the red blooming on the dog's ribs. The shot. It had been aimed at Rex. Caleb's stomach dropped.

Alana crawled over to the dog and began to assess the damage. Caleb fell to his knees beside her. The aftereffects of the incident were hitting him, adrenaline with no place to go making his hands shake and his breathing fast and shallow.

"Is he okay?" He couldn't have gotten attached to the dog already, surely, but his throat was tight. "And are you okay?"

"Give me your shirt." Alana didn't look at him, attention focused on the dog. He pulled off the shirt and handed it to her, glad that the day was warm.

Alana made a pad of the shirt and put pressure on the dog's ribs. "I need to get him to the clinic. I don't think anything major was hit, but this is going to need stitches."

Caleb glanced around. A neighbor across the street had come out, and Caleb saw a man running from the house next door. Conners—Caleb had been given a photo and he recognized the man's face.

He focused on Alana. "Can I pick him up?"

Alana nodded, looking at him for the first time since the attempted abduction. "Just let me keep pressure on the wound."

He gently slid his arms under Rex's body. The dog

whined, and Alana rested her free hand on his head for a moment.

"It's okay, baby. We're going to take care of you."

Caleb struggled to get to his feet while carrying eighty pounds of wounded dog. He'd just managed to straighten when Conners arrived at their side.

"What happened?" Fear tinged the man's voice. He must have heard the shot.

Alana was still focused on the dog. Caleb took the first steps in the direction of his SUV.

"Someone attempted to abduct Alana, and Rex went for him. There was a car, idling on the street, plate RAF 143. Someone in the car shot the dog. The attackers fled in the vehicle. We're taking Rex to be dealt with at the clinic. Can you notify the police?"

Conners nodded. Alana stared at Caleb for a moment then turned back to the dog.

At Caleb's SUV, the bag of dog food was still on the ground, the duffel bags in the back seat. Conners had pulled out a cell phone but was still close by.

"Can you clear the back seat for me, Mr. Conners?" Alana asked.

"Sure. You okay, Alana?"

She nodded. "Good enough. We can worry about me later."

Conners frowned but emptied the back seat, setting the duffels aside and moving the bag of dog food to lean on the garage door. Alana lifted her hand from the dog long enough to slide into the back seat.

"Put him back here with me."

Caleb did as she told him, and she resumed pressure. He closed the door and checked his pockets, relieved that the vehicle keys were still there. He nodded at Conners and rounded the vehicle to the driver's seat.

Alana lowered the window. "Mr. Conners—I dropped the keys to the apartment on the porch. Can you get them, after you've contacted the police?"

"Sure, and I'll take this stuff up to the apartment for safety."

"Thanks." She met Caleb's eyes in the rearview mirror. "You don't know where to go, do you?"

He shook his head. He'd been given the address before he arrived but didn't know the directions yet. Mr. Johnson wouldn't know even that much.

"Turn left once you're out of the driveway. I'll direct you as we go."

He put the keys in the ignition and glanced around. There was no sign of the car that had brought the attacker, but he kept his eyes peeled all the way to Alana's clinic. Once they arrived, he scanned the area again as he came around to carry Rex in. Nothing he could see.

Something was going on. There was no proof yet that it was connected to the jewelry store heist all those years ago, but people didn't try to abduct veterinarians in daylight for fun. Caleb suspected Yoxall was right.

Chapter Three

Until Rex was stitched up and stabilized, Alana shut everything else out of her mind. She would freak when the dog was taken care of.

The bullet had grazed the rib bones but not hit an organ or major artery. Alana almost shoved Caleb into an examination room with Rex in his arms. He stood back once Rex was on the table. Alana grabbed the supplies she needed, mostly ignoring Caleb. She couldn't totally, because he was definitely attractive and he was there, in his undershirt, after having come to her rescue and Rex's. His shirt was on the floor, soaked with Rex's blood.

Once the bleeding was staunched and the wound sterilized and sutured, Alana was able to focus on what had brought them here. She found a scrub top that belonged to one of her coworkers and passed it to Caleb. Then she leaned against the counter as everything rushed back in. Caleb's arrival, the walk with Rex, and then, out of nowhere, it seemed, someone grabbing her.

It was darker now, but it had still been daylight when the man had clamped his arms around her and started to pull her away with him. After a moment of shock, she'd tried to scream again, but he'd flattened his hand over her mouth. He was so strong that her struggles were futile. She'd felt fear, more than she had after the home invasions. Strong, paralyzing fear. She might have sent up a quick prayer, but it had all happened so fast, and been so terrifying.

Then Rex had launched into them, and Alana was no longer the one in danger. There were some scary thoughts circling about the whys of this happening, but it was easier to focus on some of the hows.

She looked up. Caleb was watching her, arms crossed over the borrowed scrubs.

"Is Rex okay?"

Alana nodded. "He will be. Some rest and recovery and he'll be good as new."

"That's a relief."

It was. But Alana had questions.

"Is Rex an attack dog?"

Caleb looked down and away from her. "I don't know a lot about him. But I think my uncle got him as a retired police dog. I don't know if he was a drug sniffer, or cadaver dog, or what."

Alana was taken aback. "All police dogs are trained for attacking and defending. If you plan to keep Rex, you need to know what he was trained for, and the commands he responds to."

Caleb sighed. "You're right. I'm just glad he was able to stop that guy from abducting you. Rex is okay, you said, but how are you?"

That was when it hit her. Someone had tried to abduct her. Had grabbed her, almost forced her against her will into a car—who knows what might have happened to her if Caleb and Rex hadn't been there? She started to shake and turned to hide her reaction from Caleb. He was a stranger, and he didn't need to witness her falling apart.

"Alana?"

Suddenly Caleb was behind her, and his size and warmth were reassuring. They made her feel safe.

She clasped her hands together to control the trembling. "I think it's just hitting me now."

She heard him sigh. "I'd suggest you just go home and relax, but the police want to talk to you."

Right. She needed to talk to them, describe what happened, and the man who'd—

A sob burst out. Caleb gently rubbed her back with one hand and comforted her as she fell apart. It had been a day.

Alana pulled in a choppy breath and swiped at her face. She was too embarrassed to look at Caleb after breaking down.

"Sorry."

"No problem. I'm happy to help. I can tell the police that you need more time."

Alana shook her head. She needed to pull herself together and do her duty. "I'll talk to them. I'm just worried about leaving Rex alone."

Caleb's voice softened. "I have a suggestion."

She turned around. "You could keep an eye on him— but no, they want to talk to you as well, don't they? Maybe I can call someone…"

"I'll ask them to come here, to the clinic. We can talk to them and still keep an eye or ear out for Rex."

Alana attempted a smile. "That would be great. I should have thought of that. I just…" She just wasn't herself, still trying to come to terms with the events of the day. Not just the day, but the past couple of weeks.

"I'll call them now, tell them you're tied up and ask them to take our statements here." He stepped away then, taking his phone from his pocket. Alana took another glance at the bandages on Rex and checked his breathing. So far, so good.

Fifteen minutes later, Alana was repeating her story to the same police officers who'd taken her previous statements about the break-ins. She'd left work, come home, taken a short walk with Caleb and Rex, gone into her house, and on the way out, the man had grabbed her.

The attacker was taller than her, maybe six feet. *Not quite as tall as Caleb*, her mind suggested, not very helpfully. Strong, ruthless. Brown eyes and hair, facial features covered so she couldn't describe them. No visible scars or tattoos. She hadn't noticed what he was wearing, except for the gloves that had been on his hands when he grabbed her and covered her mouth. Yes, he could have been the home intruder from before.

Alana hoped Caleb had been more observant.

She was no more helpful when it came to motive. It wasn't reasonable to think this and the break-ins were a coincidence, but she had no idea what the men were after. After repeating it three times, she was tired, anxious and close to losing her temper. She sent up a prayer of gratitude when the officers closed their notebooks and told her that was all for now.

She let them out the front door of the clinic. Caleb came out of the room Rex was recuperating in.

"All done?" His smile was small and sympathetic, as if he understood how she felt.

"Don't they need to speak to you?"

"A couple of guys talked to me while those two were grilling you. We'll have to sign statements tomorrow."

Alana slouched against the receptionist's counter. She glanced at her wrist. "I can't believe it's only ten p.m. It feels like the middle of the night. You must be more than ready to go."

"I can drive you back to your place."

Alana shook her head. "No, I'll stay here to keep an eye on Rex. We have a cot set up in back in case we have a patient who needs monitoring. You go ahead."

His lips pinched. "I don't want to leave you alone."

She clenched her fists, stomach churning. She hadn't thought about what it meant to be here on her own. The possibility that those men might return made her shudder. But she couldn't spend the rest of her life afraid of being alone. She pointed at the alarm beside the door.

"We've got a good security system—we have pharmaceuticals here and need to be secure for insurance purposes."

Caleb followed her finger and frowned at the display. "Still… I think I should be near Rex, too. He's my responsibility now."

Alana appreciated that Caleb took Rex's care seriously. He hadn't given the impression that he was happy about being left with the dog, but he was trying. There were a lot of good qualities to her new tenant.

"Tell you what." Caleb indicated the clinic. "Let's take turns watching Rex. We can each get a little rest. I wouldn't sleep anyway, knowing you were here on your own with him because of me."

"Hardly because of you. Because of me, or more

precisely, because of whoever was in the car shooting the gun."

Caleb rubbed the back of his neck. "Unless you'd rather not be alone with me? You don't know me after all."

Alana stilled and narrowed her eyes. She looked at the man in the doorway, whom she'd met only hours ago. It felt like so much longer.

It was true that she didn't know him. But she trusted him. He and Rex had prevented her abduction. He couldn't be involved, unless the attempted kidnapping had been set up just to make him look good, but Rex's injury made that idea a nonstarter. And something that convoluted? It was what she'd see in an action movie, not what would happen in her life. Mr. Conners had vouched for Caleb. The police hadn't suggested she stay away from him. She wasn't at risk if he stayed.

"I feel safer with you around. Since you're preventing people abducting me, rather than abducting me yourself."

Caleb smiled. He had a great smile. Alana reminded herself that wasn't why they were here. It was probably shock making her feel so close to him.

"Okay, we'll take turns with Rex. You want to rest first?"

Alana pushed herself off the desk. Her muscles were tired, but her brain was too wired to sleep. "Still too wound up for that. Would you like to?"

He shook his head. "No, I'm not ready to sleep yet."

"We've got some drinks back in the break room. And you probably haven't eaten…"

"Something to drink would be good." At that opportune moment, Caleb's stomach growled. "Can we order some food?"

Alana's stomach gurgled in response. She pushed a hand against her middle in an attempt to silence it. "Probably a good idea. You like pizza?"

His eyes opened wide. "Doesn't everyone?"

"There's a place we call for lunch sometimes—why don't you tell me what you do or don't like, and I'll get them to deliver something?"

"Hate olives, love pepperoni."

Alana reached for the phone. They had the pizzeria's phone number programmed in. "Got it. Salad? Garlic bread?"

"Yes and yes."

Alana gave him another glance. She'd order lots. They could eat leftovers later, but someone his size, as fit as he was, must eat a good amount. She didn't want him to be hungry.

"Okay. I'll call it in, and then give Rex another check."

When the pizza delivery arrived, Caleb handled the door. They ate in the reception area. The clinic break room was small, and in reception there was room to open the pizza box and salad on the magazine table.

Caleb kept his eyes on Alana. She'd been through a lot today. He wondered if taking care of Rex had helped her feel more in control, since events had been anything but.

He hadn't wanted to take on a dog, but he was grateful that Rex had been there. It gave him chills to consider what might have happened without the dog. Someone wanted something from Alana, desperately, and it could very well be related to her father.

Caleb couldn't bring it up because he wasn't supposed to know. He didn't know how much Alana knew about her father. He wished he could simply ask, but if she knew something, she might not be willing to talk about it, especially to someone she'd just met. After all, she was friendly with Conners, her neighbor and a cop, and hadn't told him anything.

Over pizza he asked her why she became a vet. Her mother had worked at this clinic as a receptionist, and Alana had spent a lot of time here. She loved animals and wanted to care for them. She hadn't been misled by any romantic ideals of the life. She'd seen what the vet had done and knew that helping animals sometimes involved causing temporary pain. She was willing to do that, even though the animals might not like her as a result.

"But you don't have any pets?"

She blinked her eyes and started to tidy up their mess. "We had a dog, but she died not long after my mother passed, and I just haven't been able to handle getting another one. Not yet. I'm still grieving. Once that's over, I'll find a rescue. We do work for the local humane society, so one day I'll keep one that comes through here."

She stood with the pizza box. Caleb picked up the leftover salad and garlic bread and followed her into the break room. She put the leftovers in the fridge, and he tore up the packaging to fit in the recycling. He turned to ask if she wanted to rest now and found her staring at the wall.

He reached out a hand and gently touched her arm. "You okay?"

She startled and he moved his hand back. "Sorry. Thoughts were just miles away."

"That's okay. Anything I can help with?"

She ran a hand over her hair, smoothing the strands that had escaped the ponytail. "I just want to figure out what this is all about. There's a reason this is happening, and I should know what it is."

Caleb held his breath. Would she be willing to confide in him, this quickly?

She sat on one of the two chairs in the room. Caleb leaned against the doorframe, not speaking, trying to offer silent comfort.

"This isn't the first incident."

Caleb knew, but merely offered a grunt in his throat to say he was listening.

"There was a break-in at the house a couple of weeks ago. The door wasn't locked when I got home, and I almost thought I'd accidentally left it open, but some things were moved around. Papers mostly.

"Then I got home after work about a week later and the door was open. The house was ransacked. There was a man inside, with a mask. He ran toward me, or the door, and I turned and fell, hitting my head."

She swept back her bangs, and he saw the remnants of a bruise. His hands clenched into fists, and he fought back the anger. He knew all this, so there was no reason to be experiencing this visceral reaction.

"Those I could write off as coincidences, or a thief, but today was different. That was an attack against me, personally, and I should know why, shouldn't I?"

She sounded honest, sincere and perplexed. He believed her, that she didn't know. But maybe she knew something, something she just didn't know she knew.

"Could there be anything in the house?" Obviously, whoever was doing this believed there was, since they'd started with a break-in.

"Mom bought the house when we moved here, after Dad died. I was four. I don't remember living anywhere else. I can't imagine there's anything there that someone would want after all this time has passed. And the previous owners still live here, in a condo downtown. Mr. Conners asked them if they knew any reason someone would want to break into the house after the second incident. They had no idea. They bought the house new about twenty years before they sold it to Mom.

"I've tried to think of something, but it's not like the place has a priest's hole, or secret passages. It's just a normal house, with normal people living in it. There was no mystery about Mom or me."

Caleb could ask about the previous owners, but Conners had already checked, so he didn't think that would lead anywhere. Did Alana really think she and her mother had been normal?

Normal people weren't in witness protection.

"No one has bothered the Gayners, the previous owners, at their condo. So it's not them. But I can't think of anything about my family that would cause this. I was born in Toronto, but I don't remember any of that. My dad died in a car accident when I was four, and Mom moved here and bought the house with the insurance money. She worked for the vet, I went to WCVM in Saskatoon for my degree and came back here."

Caleb checked her face, her body language. From everything he could see, she wasn't lying. Had no one told her about her family and their history before they moved here? Did she not know she and her mom were in WitPro? If he asked her, she'd want to know how he knew, and that would blow his cover.

He swallowed. "Was anyone else involved in your dad's accident that might explain this?"

Her father had died in prison. Not when Alana was four years old, but when she was seventeen.

Alana's shoe nudged the linoleum in front of her. "Mom said he fell asleep at the wheel and hit a tree. No one else involved. And Mom died after her second stroke. Nobody involved in that, either."

That he knew was true. "The rest of your family?"

She looked up at him. "There is no one. Mom and Dad were only children, and their parents died before I was born. I have nothing. I mean, nothing to explain this. Which makes me think it has to be random, but that doesn't make sense, either."

Nothing she said was true, but she spoke like she believed it, like it was truth.

What do I do here, Lord?

He wanted to tell her what the real issue was and see how she reacted. If she would be shocked by the content of what he said, or just that he knew. But that wasn't his job. How could they discover what was happening when he couldn't ask her about what he knew was probably the cause?

Before he had a chance to break cover, and blurt out something he shouldn't, Alana asked him a question.

"Do you think there could be anything in my mother's safety deposit box? Something that might be what these people are after?"

Chapter Four

She'd surprised Caleb. His eyes widened and his jaw dropped. "Your mother has a safety deposit box? I mean, she had?"

Alana felt silly and obligated to defend herself. Having a safety deposit box wasn't that unusual. That Alana hadn't checked it after her mother died…maybe that was.

"I never thought much about it. We didn't have valuables to store. And when she died, I dealt with things by keeping busy—making lists of what I had to do, so I didn't feel anything, you know?"

She wasn't sure he did understand, but he nodded, and no longer looked stunned at what she'd said.

"She had a key to a safety deposit box in her things, and I assumed it was for her will, or insurance. But before I had a chance to check it out, our lawyer called to say that he had all those papers in his office. By then, the funeral was over, most of my list was done, and it hit me, really hit me, that she was gone."

Alana wrapped her arms around her waist. The grief still gripped her, out of the blue, reminding her that she was alone. No, not alone. She had God. But her family was gone.

"I forgot about the box. There was nothing missing in the paperwork, so I assumed it was empty. That she'd taken the paperwork to the lawyer and didn't return the key to the bank before she died."

Caleb reached out a hand, offering comfort. Alana clung to it tightly.

"Maybe it is empty. But you might as well check to be sure that there's nothing there to explain what's happening."

Alana nodded. It was the smart thing to do, and she was a smart person. But there was an unexpected reluctance to go and open the box. It was the last opportunity to find a communication from her mother. There was probably nothing, but if she opened the box and saw the emptiness, then that would be it. Her mother was gone.

She didn't have the luxury of ignoring it now. Things were happening, and people and animals were either hurt or getting hurt. And if something in that box could explain it, or was what they were searching for, she had to find out.

She had a difficult time believing there would be anything. If there was nothing, then what had happened must be random violence or mistaken identity. Surely they'd stop.

She released a long breath. "I'll go tomorrow. On my lunch break."

Caleb's brow creased. "You're working tomorrow? After staying up like this?"

That teased a smile from her. "I told you, there's a cot I can sleep on. This won't be the first time I've kept watch over a patient, and I've been able to work the next day."

Caleb still looked concerned, which was sweet.

"I can ask Mauve to see if she can reschedule some clients, and maybe I can take the afternoon off."

Caleb hmmed. "That sounds like a good idea, but I'm still worried about you. After today…"

Alana opened her mouth, ready to refute the implication that there was any risk in going about her day, but she had almost been abducted.

"I can't hole up in my house indefinitely." She had her work, her life—and it still wasn't proven that she was the object of whatever was going on. She was probably in denial, but she would really like to think these people had made a mistake. Of course, she didn't want them to go after anyone else, either.

"What if I go with you?"

Her first instinct was to refuse. She wasn't used to asking for help, not for something like this. She didn't know Caleb. They'd only just met. But he *had* helped her already. Mr. Conners said he'd been in the army, so he knew about handling violence.

As if he could sense the war in her thoughts, he continued, "I don't have to go into the bank with you. I'll just drive over, walk in with you, then walk you out. I can bring my gun—I have a permit—but hopefully we won't need it. If there's a chance these people are after you or anything that might be in that box, and they're using weapons, I'd like to know I had something to protect you with as well."

Alana hated that she wanted to say yes, put the whole thing in his hands. She could give him the key, let him go to the bank while she stayed locked in her house.

But no, she refused to give in to fear. And she doubted
the bank would let him in anyway. She could give in to
his request and have someone with her. It would be nice
not to feel alone again, even just for a short while. She'd
lost touch with friends while caring for her mother and
had been slow to reach out again since.

"Okay, that sounds like a plan. It's probably nothing."

"Probably," Caleb agreed. But something—his expression, tone, stance—told her that he didn't believe
it was nothing.

That worried her.

Caleb insisted on sleeping on the couch in the waiting room. Alana checked on Rex, then stretched out
on the cot to try to sleep.

Her thoughts circled from Caleb to the abduction
to Rex to her mother and what might be in that safety
deposit box. She wasn't trusting God, relying too much
on herself. She mentally recited Psalm 23, her mother's
favorite, and finally managed a restless sleep.

She had scrubs and a change of underwear here for
times like this, and there was a shower in the bathroom, since work could get messy. Alana was able to
clean up, and fresh clothes made a world of difference
to her outlook. Caleb disappeared as soon as Mauve
arrived, and Alana was left to make explanations to
her coworkers.

The morning dragged, partly because she was tired
and partly because she was waiting for her lunch break.
The chance of finding the answer to everything that
was going on was close to nil, but at least she was *doing*
something. She'd see Caleb again, and that hit her right

in the feels. She hadn't responded to a man like this in forever.

She wondered if he'd be interested in spending time with her. According to Mr. Conners, Caleb attended a church like theirs, and might be attending her church while he was here. Surely that meant they had a basic shared belief system. Enough to start a friendship, and that might lead to more.

Alana had been waiting to take a dog's temperature for a couple of minutes and shook those thoughts away.

When lunchtime finally dragged around, she was tempted to change out of her scrubs. She wouldn't normally do that in the middle of the day, even for a trip to the bank. This was a tight-knit community within the larger city of Winnipeg, and there were few strangers. People at the bank would know she was the local vet, and not think twice about seeing her in scrubs.

It wasn't them she was thinking about.

Since she had nothing suitable to change into, she stayed in her scrubs. Once she'd finished with her last patient of the day and completed her notes, she came back to the reception area and found Caleb waiting for her. The smile that crossed his face when he saw her banished thoughts of clothes from her mind.

Alana had brought her purse with her last night so she could get into the clinic. She'd put the key to the safety deposit box on her key chain when she'd found it in her mother's possessions after her death, and had her passport for identification, in case a driver's license wasn't enough. She'd gone to a conference in Minneapolis last month, and had needed the passport to cross the border. She was ready for the bank and hoped that

Caleb might consider having lunch together after that visit. It would be a way to thank him for helping her.

She'd rescheduled her afternoon as she'd told him she'd do, so lunch could linger if they wished. If Caleb didn't have to be somewhere.

"I'm ready. Rex is doing well, and you should be able to take him home tomorrow."

Caleb nodded. "That's good. I brought my SUV in case he was ready—want to take that?"

"Do you know where the bank is?"

He grinned. "I looked it up on my phone. It's close by."

"I usually walk, if I need to use the ATM or something. The clinic banks there, as well as my mom and me. Just me, now."

Caleb's smile vanished. "I don't think walking's a good idea."

He was being overcautious, because what could happen on a street full of people? She was willing to indulge him, since it meant they'd travel together. They could still go for lunch after. "Then your vehicle it is."

The bank had a parking lot, so parking wouldn't be an issue. She'd miss a chance to get some exercise, but she was tired.

Caleb opened the door to the clinic for her but scanned the street before letting her pass through. He held open the passenger door as well, but the way he kept looking around indicated it was more for protection than chivalry. Maybe it was both.

Within five minutes, they were walking through the front door of the local branch of her bank. She smiled and waved at one of the tellers, a member of her church.

She headed to the customer service desk, where another familiar face waited.

"Hello, Julie. Everything ready?" Alana had called ahead to make sure she could get into the box. Since she and her mother had their accounts at this branch, she'd already filed all the paperwork about her mother's death. Alana just needed the key.

"Everything is set up for you. You doing okay, sweetie?"

Alana smiled and nodded but didn't tell Julie about the excitement of the past couple of weeks. No need to spread the news if it wasn't already out there.

Julie slid over a sign-in sheet. "I need your signature, and some identification. Is your friend going in as well?" Julie stared at him with curiosity.

Caleb shook his head and walked over to the seats set up for people waiting for appointments.

"Who's that?" Julie asked in a whisper as Alana pulled out her passport and driver's license.

"That's my new tenant. Can I get into the box now?" Alana sounded abrupt, but she didn't want to start any gossip about Caleb.

"Right this way." Julie stood and led the way to the vault. She verified the box number and put her key in the lock, then waited while Alana inserted and turned hers.

"You bring the box with you—we have a room for you to check out the contents. There's no waste basket there, so everything you take in needs to come out with you."

Alana was surprised at the level of security. Some people must have valuables in their boxes. She followed Julie to a small room with a table and chair and set the box down.

Julie left, telling Alana to call her when she was done.

For a moment, Alana just looked at the box. It was three inches deep, ten inches wide, and almost two feet long. Not that big. There couldn't be much in there, if anything.

She was reluctant to open it. At this moment, there were no surprises, no reasons someone would be after her. The events of the last couple of weeks were random, not intentional, and they could end as abruptly as they began. Unless there was something in this box, something that would provide a reason for the attacks. If so, her life was going to change. She didn't want that.

She shook her head. There wasn't anything inside. She was worried about nothing. She was just closing a false door, making sure there was nothing left to explain. Still, her hand was trembling when she laid it on the box. She released a quick prayer and pulled the lid up.

The box wasn't empty.

There were papers inside, a couple of old brown legal envelopes and a bunch of yellowed letters wrapped in an elastic. The letters were addressed to a woman she didn't know, didn't think her mother knew. Marie Campbell.

Her brow furrowed. The legal envelopes were also headed with the other woman's name. She carefully picked up the batch of letters and set them aside. The two envelopes remaining held something, though nothing heavy. They'd been sealed at some point, but the flap was tucked inside, nothing preventing Alana from looking at the contents.

She slipped the tab clear and shook the contents out onto the table in front of her. A passport. Driver's license. Two birth certificates. One social insurance number card.

She picked up the driver's license. The name was the same as on the envelopes. Marie Campbell. The photo was old and hard to decipher, but the woman looked to be in her late twenties. She resembled her mother. A relative? Sister? But her mother had no siblings.

One birth certificate belonged to the same woman. The birth date was exactly the same as her mother's. A twin sister? Had something terrible happened to her?

The other birth certificate was for someone younger. Much younger. Alana blinked at the birth date. It was the same as hers, but the name was Amanda Campbell.

She shoved aside the social insurance card, since it was nothing but a name and numbers. She picked up the passport, flipped it open and found the page with the photo.

The passport was dated from almost thirty years ago. But the photo was much clearer than the driver's license. The eyes staring out of the photo were familiar, as was the whole face, though younger than Alana's memories. It was her mother, or her identical twin.

An identical twin, Marie Campbell, with a daughter born the same day as Alana?

Alana shivered and shoved everything back in the envelope.

She wanted to go back an hour, never come to the bank, never open this box.

But she had.

Chapter Five

As soon as Alana came out from the rooms in the back of the bank, Caleb knew the safety deposit box had something in it. She had her hands wrapped around a couple of envelopes, and a shell-shocked expression on her face. She barely smiled at the woman, Julie, whom she'd been so friendly with before she opened the box.

He stood and crossed into her path. She looked up, eyes widening, as if she'd forgotten he was waiting for her.

"Hey there, are you okay?"

Caleb wasn't sure exactly what she'd found, but he suspected it related to her past life, before she and her mother entered into witness protection. It was possible Alana had never learned about that, and this expression on her face? Looked like something had affected her deeply.

He wanted to know what she'd found, but he also wanted to be sure she was okay. He wasn't feigning the concern in his voice. Or his heart.

Alana blinked and swallowed. "The box wasn't empty. Can we go home?"

Caleb wrapped his arm around her shoulders, and she relaxed into him. "Sure. You got something to put that stuff into? Just in case someone is looking for it?"

She stiffened under his arm. Had she forgotten the reason she'd come to check out the box? She shuddered, then reached for her purse.

"I have a reusable shopping bag."

"Great."

Alana's hands trembled as she pulled open her purse.

"May I help? I can hold this stuff while you find your shopping bag."

She paused. Caleb wondered if she didn't want him to touch the paperwork. If she'd found something so big, so shocking, that she didn't trust him.

He dropped his shoulders and stepped back from her. Ideally, he would have time to earn her trust before anything this big came up, but he didn't have that luxury. If she wanted to shut him out, he couldn't push her without revealing his real identity.

Not possible. This was his chance to carry on what his dad had wanted to do before he'd been injured, what his grandfather had done. If he couldn't maintain his cover with Alana, a veterinarian with no criminal ties anyone knew of, how would he handle a real and challenging case?

Telling her might put her at risk, if she avoided him.

Alana drew a breath and passed him the papers. He drew in a breath, shocked by her trust. Dropping his gaze for just a moment, he clenched his jaw when he saw the name on the envelopes. Marie Campbell. Her mother's name. Her name before WitPro.

Alana managed to pull out a cloth shopping bag.

She held it open, and he carefully dropped the papers inside.

"Hold that closely under your arm, and we'll get you home."

Alana nodded and tucked the bag tight to her body. Her eyes raced over the people around her in the bank. Yes, it had been something big she'd found. Something that had spooked her badly.

Caleb stepped ahead of her, heading to the door and his vehicle outside. He checked for anyone looking or behaving suspiciously. There were a couple of parked vehicles with people inside, but he didn't know the area or the residents and didn't know if they were potential problems.

Alana stayed close behind him, following until they got to his SUV and he opened the door for her. She dropped the bag and purse on the floor, and once she was seated, he closed the door. He moved around the vehicle, still checking their surroundings, and got in on the driver's side. Her hands gripped the seat belt.

"Let's get you home."

She nodded. He pulled out of the lot, watching for anyone following. He didn't see anything, but it wasn't like Alana's home address was a secret to whoever was after her.

Caleb pulled into the driveway of Alana's house, beside her car, still parked where she'd left it when she got home from work yesterday. He'd driven her with the wounded Rex to the clinic, and this was the first she'd been home since. It seemed like more than a day had passed. He turned the vehicle off and waited for her to decide what she was going to do.

He'd like to know what was in the papers she'd

found. Depending on what it was, it might be something he needed to know to protect her. But he couldn't tell her that without looking suspicious. It was none of Caleb *Johnson's* problem.

"I can walk you to your door. You said you have a good alarm, right?"

She nodded. "Um, would you mind coming in with me? I can make us something to eat."

"Are you sure? You look like you've had a shock." Caleb wished he could be the person she thought he was. A new acquaintance with no agenda but to help. He didn't want to know so much about her past before she decided to share with him. He didn't like feeling that comforting her was using her, taking advantage.

Alana stared down at the bag and purse in the floor of his vehicle.

"It has been a shock. I'm not sure I want to be alone." Her brown eyes turned to him. "I'm sorry, I know you just got here, and your dog is injured, and you don't really know me, but you feel like someone safe, and if you don't mind I'd like you to stay."

Caleb had forgotten about Rex, but he didn't mention that. His focus had been on Alana. He wasn't used to being responsible for an animal.

"I'd be happy to keep you company. And I'm a lousy cook, so…"

A smile curved her lips, before her worries drew her mouth down again. He felt good that he'd lightened things for her, even if it was just for a moment.

"Don't get too excited. I'm thinking of sandwiches. That okay?"

He nodded, and she reached for the door handle. Caleb put a hand on her shoulder. "Let me go first."

Alana bit her lip. "But that's not fair. If someone is out there—"

"If someone is out there, and they're after you, they're not going to try to abduct me. I've had training. I was in the army. I'm better prepared for this than you."

She still looked worried, but he opened his door after checking the rearview mirror and slid out, looking for cars parked on the street, or people loitering. It was early in the afternoon, and the neighborhood was quiet. He came around to Alana's door and opened it for her, shielding her with his own body.

That felt right and natural.

She smiled up at him as she exited the car. She leaned down to pick up the bags, and this time he let her lead the way to her front door, while he continued to watch the area. Nothing looked out of place, nothing suspicious. But he couldn't relax.

Alana turned the key in the lock and opened the door. She punched the keypad by the door and drew in a long, shuddering breath. Caleb followed her in and closed the door, turning the dead bolt.

"Want to arm it again?"

She did. Caleb noted the code, and also that she didn't try to hide it from him. She was too trusting, but he memorized the digits, in case he needed them in future. Then he turned to examine her home.

It was an older house, not as open as new builds, but the colors were warm and welcoming, the furniture comfortable-looking and slightly worn. He followed Alana down a hall and through an opening into the kitchen. The kitchen had been updated, but not for a while. The cupboards were painted a warm cream color, and the counter was stone. She dropped the bags on a farm table that served as an eating area, and turned to face him.

"I just realized it's not even that late in the afternoon. It feels like hours have gone by since I left the clinic."

Caleb rested a hip on the kitchen counter. "It does, doesn't it? What do you want to do? Eat? Take a nap? Watch TV?"

If she napped, he might be able to look over the papers she'd found. Again, a frisson of discomfort climbed up his spine. He needed to get over this when he was undercover. He wasn't going to destroy her papers, he just wanted to know what they were and if they provided the evidence needed to reveal the truth about what happened twenty-five years ago. There was no videotape, and no jewelry in envelopes that flat, so this might not be what Yoxall was looking for. Maybe the break-ins and the abduction were about something else. Something random or connected to her life in a way they hadn't discovered.

"You must be hungry, and I should be. I'll put together some food, and then…would you like a drink? I don't think I can nap or relax in front of the TV till I've gone through—that." She waved a hand at the shopping bag on the table.

"Sure. How can I help?"

"Just stay here. It's weird, I know, but having you here feels like it's protecting me from whatever is in those papers. I'll only be a couple of minutes with the food."

Caleb sat, the envelopes beside him. He was itching to open them, see if there were clues to where the evidence might be. Information about what had happened to his dad's friend all those years ago. His father was the person he respected most, and he wanted to make him proud and help him understand the events from the past.

Caleb restrained himself and, instead, thought of ways he might be able to see what the contents were without Alana knowing. He had the alarm code. He could come back in when Alana was at work. He could plan something with Conners.

While his mind plotted, he watched Alana move around the kitchen, slicing bread, taking things out of the fridge, finally coming back with a plate of sandwiches.

"Thanks. I need to stock the apartment with food."

Alana put plates and glasses in front of them. She paused, a frown crossing her face.

"I'm sorry, I'm taking you away from your own plans."

Caleb rested a hand on her forearm. "You were up last night taking care of my dog. I owe you. And I couldn't rest easy if I thought those men might try to take you again."

Alana drew in a breath and sat beside him. "Selfishly, I'm not going to argue that you should go. I need to look at this stuff, and I'm afraid it might prove that this all wasn't random."

"Can I help?" He repeated his offer.

She smiled. It wasn't a great smile, but she had made an effort.

"Eat a sandwich, let me focus my brain, and keep me company. That's all I need right now."

Caleb's stomach gurgled, like it had the previous night, not following with the drama and demanding attention. They laughed, a release to the tension.

"Eat." Alana indicated the plate.

"Only if you do, too."

Alana took a sandwich, and Caleb grabbed two. His body was reminding him to eat after all. He paused. "Do you want to say grace?"

Alana nodded. Caleb dropped his head and said a short prayer, offering thanks for the food and asking for guidance.

"Thank you."

He still waited to eat.

She frowned at him. "Is something wrong?"

"Just making sure you eat as well."

Alana huffed then took a bite. "Happy?"

"Yep."

Caleb took a much larger bite. He chewed and swallowed. "These are good."

"Thanks. My mom made her own mustard—swore it was better than store-bought."

Her smile dropped and she stared again at the envelopes.

"I'm not sure I even knew her."

Caleb jerked his head toward the envelopes. "Something in there?"

"Yeah. Sorry, I can't eat now." She pushed the plate away.

Caleb quickly swallowed the last of the food he'd taken. "Understandable. If you tell me where your TV is, I could go watch something while you deal with that."

Alana bit her lip again.

"Would you mind being my sounding board? I'm trying to figure out what these papers are and what they mean, and I don't want to jump to crazy conclusions. Right now, I'm imagining things that would be at home in a thriller or spy story, and another person processing this might keep me from getting carried away."

Caleb couldn't have come up with a more ideal scenario if he'd been scripting it, and again, it made him feel dirty. Guilty. But he'd offered to leave her alone and she'd asked him to stay. He needed to do his job. Because, in the long run, that was what would keep Alana safe.

"Sure, I'd be happy to help. What do you want me to do?"

Alana poured them each a glass of lemonade. He thought she was still procrastinating the moment she'd need to face what she'd found. She left for a moment, returning with a notepad and pens and a laptop.

She passed him the notepad and a pen before sitting down.

"I'll tell you what I've found, and you note down what seems important. And if we need to look things up, we've got the internet. Maybe we can solve the mystery of Marie Campbell, and why she looks just like my mother."

Chapter Six

Alana dumped out one envelope. Passport, driver's license, two birth certificates and a social insurance card. Caleb refrained with difficulty from grabbing and opening the passport, mentally noting the information on the fronts of the documents. Marie Campbell, and the second birth certificate was in the name of Amanda Campbell. Alana's name, before the jewelry store heist, the dead cop and witness protection. He worked to keep his expression from changing, but she wasn't looking at him.

Alana arranged the papers on the table. "Marie Campbell has the same birth date as my mother. And the passport—" She opened it up and showed him. "That photo looks just like my mother did in the earliest pictures I have of her. Amanda Campbell has my birth date."

Alana let the passport fall shut and breathed out.

"Possibility one, my mother had an identical twin she never told me about, and that twin had a daughter born on the same date as me."

Caleb wasn't sure how to respond.

Alana continued. "Or two, Marie Campbell is my mother, and I'm Amanda Campbell, and my mother forged documents about us. Was she a criminal? Am I?"

Alana's eyes were wide, and her brow furrowed. She blinked, and Caleb sensed she was on the verge of tears. He wanted to reassure her. She and her mother weren't criminals. But he wasn't supposed to know this. His urge to comfort battled with his mission.

His eyes caught the other papers she'd found. Surely, if Marie Campbell had kept these identification documents she'd have kept more. Something that might explain the truth to Alana.

"Don't leap to conclusions. Maybe you should check the rest of this stuff. Or look up Marie Campbell on the internet—see what you can find about her." Caleb didn't know what there would be to find. Not much after the trial, unless Alana had skills in digging up data. People in WitPro were supposed to be protected, and he was pretty sure their online presence was scrubbed.

Alana drew in a long breath and ran a finger over the other envelope with the name Marie Campbell written on it. Every delay proved her reluctance. This was a lot for her to take in, so maybe she was overwhelmed. Or maybe she wanted to be alone. Caleb who had a job to do needed to stay close, but Caleb who worried about Alana was ready to give her space.

"Would you like me to go?"

Her head jerked sideways, an emphatic no. Whether for protection against physical threats, or just those posed by the contents of her mother's safety deposit box, he wasn't sure. But he stayed, quietly, giving Alana the time to work this through.

She finally took the second envelope and drew it close. Again, she flipped open the flap and tipped it upside down. Newspaper clippings scattered over the kitchen tabletop. There was also a smaller, letter-sized envelope, the outside worn but unaddressed. Caleb kept his hands off the contents of that envelope with an effort.

Alana flipped the clippings over, sorting them by date. Caleb caught bits of the headlines, including words like *Jewelry*, *Death* and *Police officer*. These must be articles covering the case and trial in which Alana and her family were involved.

Once they were organized, Alana smoothed the pile. She looked over at Caleb. "Would you like to read this as well?"

Yes. He had to be careful that he didn't reveal any information not in the clippings.

"Would you like me to?"

She glanced down at the yellowed clippings. "Probably good to have an outside opinion on what I find. If you don't mind."

He didn't.

Alana read the first clipping, and then passed it over to him. It was from a Toronto paper and indicated that an off-duty police officer had been found dead in a jewelry store, presumably attempting to halt a robbery. The second clipping started to expose the ugly truth. The jeweler, Greg Campbell, had been detained. There were no signs of a robbery.

Alana's posture grew more and more rigid with each article. She didn't stop, however, or take a break. She followed the story through the arrest, trial and conviction.

The details in the stories, all from Toronto papers, followed the narrative Caleb had been given. Greg Campbell, the jeweler, had been suspected of fencing stolen goods. The policeman, Walter Abbott, had offered him a deal instead of arresting him. They would fake a robbery, and Abbott and Campbell would split the proceeds from selling the stolen merchandise, and the money from the insurance claim.

There was an altercation, the details of which were still a mystery, since Campbell didn't speak in his defense. Instead, his wife, Marie Campbell, had testified about the plan to fake a robbery and claim insurance. Campbell was convicted for the fencing, the attempted theft and claim, and the death of Walter Abbott. That was where the clippings stopped. Nothing in there about the other cop, the factor that made witness protection necessary.

Once Caleb had read the last one, he looked at Alana. She had been watching him, waiting for him to catch up.

"So, my father was a criminal. He didn't die, he went to prison."

Caleb rested a hand on Alana's. It was rigid and tense, but she didn't move away from the comfort he offered. "That has no reflection on you."

"Mom and I moved away and changed our names. Would she have done that on her own, or was it some kind of deal she made?"

It was a deal, but Caleb shouldn't know that. "Does it matter?"

Alana huffed a breath and looked around the house. "Our whole lives are a lie. I'm struggling with that. Why didn't she tell me? Sure, not when it happened, when I was a kid, but I've been an adult for a long time."

Caleb had no answers. He wasn't sure they'd ever know what had been going through Marie's mind. "Maybe she was embarrassed? Or didn't know how to tell you?"

Alana shook her head. "I'll never know. This whole big thing… My life is a lie, and I'll never know."

"Hey." Caleb waited until Alana looked at him again. "Your whole life isn't a lie. Your friends, your neighbors and coworkers, they all know and like the person you are, not the name you have. You're a veterinarian. That doesn't change because of this. You still help and care for animals…like Rex."

He squeezed her hand. "Maybe you need to look through the rest of it. Take your time, if necessary, but it's possible your mother left something to explain."

Like what had happened to the missing jewelry. Maybe a videotape. Any evidence that would indict someone else, and explain why someone had come after Alana's home, and now Alana herself.

Alana grabbed the blank envelope. "I hope she did, because I have a lot of questions. And anger."

The envelope contained a letter. Alana opened it up, but it wasn't addressed to her. It wasn't an explanation to Alana for why her mother had kept her secrets. It didn't even have a name it was addressed to or from.

Husband
I don't know if I'll ever send this, but I have no one to talk to. Right now, I'm sitting in my new kitchen, with my new name and my daughter who is struggling to answer to her new name. I'm

alone, except for her, and I'm so angry that we aren't together, that you did something so stupid and selfish. And we are paying for it.

As far as I can tell, Amanda and I are safe in our new identities in witness protection. I've seen no signs of someone following, or checking my mail, or being too friendly. I still don't trust anyone, and I blame you for that. I trusted you, and you risked us for money. We were worth so much more than any amount of cash you would have made.

I'm writing this so that if something happens to me, and this information becomes important, this letter will go to you and you will need to decide what to do. For safety, I have moved the package you hid. I could not be sure that you wouldn't be compelled to reveal where you'd hidden it, and I was not willing to trust you to keep us safe any longer.

If something happens, and you need to find it, I've hidden it where we had our first and last date. The last place the two of us went together for fun, while my parents took care of Amanda. Stupidly sentimental, you might think, but it was the safest place I could think of. If something happens to me, and this comes to you, protect Amanda. Do a better job than you did before you went away from us.

I do not expect to see you again. I will do my best to make a good life for Amanda—I will not send our new names because her safety is more important to me than anything else. I pray that someday I may be able to forgive you for what you've done.

Take care of our daughter, if this becomes your responsibility again.
Wife.

Caleb read the letter over Alana's shoulder.

"Is that your mother's handwriting?"

She nodded. Her eyes blinked quickly, and she swallowed hard. This had to be incredibly difficult for her, and she had no support other than him. When he heard a sob escape her rigid control, he turned and wrapped her in his arms. Maybe he was being too forward, but she gripped his shirt in her hands, and cried.

Alana finally wrestled back control over her emotions. Caleb's shirt was wet from her tears, and she drew away, wiping her eyes with the back of her hand. "Sorry about that."

He moved, giving her room to regroup. "Don't worry. This is a lot to have thrown at you all at once."

Alana tried a watery smile. "When I imagine myself in some big adventure, I never cry. I'm always strong and brave, and I thought I would be in real life, too."

Caleb smoothed a comforting hand down her arm. "You are strong and brave. But you're also a person, and unlike a movie character, you have feelings. It's okay to express them."

She sniffed. "I expressed them all over your shirt."

"Ah, shirts dry. Are you feeling better?"

"I think so. I might as well look at those last letters. Get it all over with at once."

Caleb nodded. He looked pleased and she wondered

if he liked women crying all over him. The thought of someone else being comforted like that made her skin twitch. She shoved the thought away and pulled the pile of letters over.

They were wrapped in an elastic, stiff with age. There was a piece of paper folded on top of them, and Alana pulled it out to check it first.

It was a notice from the department of corrections, telling Marie Campbell that these were the personal effects of her husband, delivered to her following his death.

So. She was an orphan. She'd thought she was, but she also thought she'd always been Alana. Amanda Campbell was also an orphan. She wondered when her mother had learned that Greg Campbell had died, and if she'd been upset, and Alana had never known.

She opened the top letter. It was addressed to Marie. There was no stamp, no address, no indication that it had ever been mailed. When she pulled out the contents, she found a short letter. Three paragraphs of love and regret and apologies for what he'd done.

She passed it to Caleb and opened the second. It was the same. There were ten letters, written over the course of five years, and they were almost identical.

Alana blinked back tears. She had cried enough on Caleb.

Caleb finished the last letter and passed it back to her. She wrapped them all back in the elastic and arranged the stacks and sheets of paper in neat piles. She tapped them with one finger.

"So, is this why someone is after me?"

It didn't seem possible. An old crime. Her father, a criminal, had gone to prison for what he'd done and, according to the department of corrections, died of cancer while serving his sentence. No indication of foul play. It was years ago. Why would anyone care about it now?

Caleb shrugged. "There isn't anything else, right? You couldn't come up with a reason until now. Suddenly you've found out a big secret from your parents' past. It makes sense that this could be the catalyst for what's happening. Maybe there's something else about this? Are there any other papers?"

Alana shook her head. "It's just…overwhelming. This—" she tapped the letters and paperwork in front of her "—is too much on its own. To find out that Mom and I had previous identities, and that we've been in hiding for most of my life? That's a lot. But to have that possibly making me a target? I can't get my mind to accept that. I need to think. Do more research, find out if this is the reason."

"Tell me how I can help."

Alana felt the smile trembling on her lips. Caleb was offering comfort and support, and she had to believe that God had sent him to help her get through this.

"Thank you, Caleb. You're already helping, just being here and supporting me. What should I do now? Do I tell the police? Do I give them these papers? Would they already know about it?"

Caleb looked away from her, and she was afraid she'd asked too much. He'd just arrived, looking for quiet to do his research. He didn't need her chaos.

But then he turned back to her. "I don't think the police know about this. If your identity was known to the entire department, you wouldn't be safe. And if an entire department knew, I think the officers would have mentioned it when all this came up, the break-ins and the abduction. Asked if that was a factor. Maybe it would be good to take it to them, and they can find out if there's more to the story."

Alana nodded. He was right. She could take the papers to the police, let them do their job, and with this gone from her possession, surely she'd be safe. If this was what her intruder/abductors wanted, they'd no longer be after her if she didn't have it.

"That's a good point. If this is what those people are after, they'll leave me alone once I don't have it anymore, right?"

Caleb frowned. Alana tilted her head, watching him. "Right?"

"It depends on whether they think you've given the police everything."

Alana's mouth started to drop. "But...this is all I have."

Caleb rubbed a hand on her arm again. "I know, and we'll have to make sure that everyone publicly knows it, too."

Why had God allowed things to fall out this way? She needed to flex her faith muscles and trust that this was all working out for good. She would. It wasn't going to be easy, though.

She took another look at the papers. "I'll get them back sometime, right?"

Caleb nodded. "Once the case is settled, yes. Do you want to make copies?"

"I do, yes. But then, if I have copies, they, whoever wants them, might still come for the copies, wouldn't they?"

Caleb's brow creased. "Maybe the police would

make copies for you and hold them until you know it's safe to keep them here."

Yes. That would work. The letters her father had written were all she had of him. She wanted to read them slowly, try to understand the man who'd been her father.

She had no idea if she knew him at all. Her mother had sometimes spoken of him. She'd shared stories of what he'd been like and what they'd done together as a family, back before he'd died. Or, more accurately, been imprisoned. She didn't know if any of those stories were true. And maybe she'd never know, but she could try to see if the man her mother had spoken of, with an affection that wasn't in the letter she'd left behind, might be the real man, the one who'd written these letters she had here.

"I like that idea. And I want to do it now. Before anything else happens."

She pushed back her chair and began to pile the papers into one stack. There wasn't that much, when all was said and done, not a lot to have upturned her world.

"Do you want to change first?"

Alana paused and looked down at her scrubs. Normally she changed as soon as she got home. She'd forgotten, focused on the envelopes she'd found.

"Of course. It won't take me long—I'll take a quick shower and be out as soon as I can."

Caleb smiled at her. "Take what time you want. I can catch up on a couple of emails, and guard this for you till you're back."

"Thank you. I really appreciate all you've done for me."

Caleb looked down. "It's nothing, really. No trouble at all."

Alana wanted to tell him it was something. That it meant a lot to her, but he didn't look like he wanted the compliments. She left him to play with his phone and went to her room feeling less burdened than she had since she'd seen the first documents.

This would all be over once she'd delivered the paperwork to the police.

Chapter Seven

Caleb watched until Alana was out of sight. After her door closed, he stood and waited at the end of the hallway until he heard the shower turn on. Taking quiet, careful steps, he returned to the pile of papers, pulling out his phone and snapping a shot of the order Alana had left them in.

Then, quickly and carefully, he pulled each item out, and took a photo of it.

He didn't want her to know what he was doing. If something happened, he could share the copies with Alana, but if she was pressured, she could say with total honesty that she didn't have copies. And he needed to send this information to Yoxall, to see if there was information coded in the letters to help them find the videotape and jewelry, and anything else the Campbells might have hidden.

He hoped doing this would protect Alana, but he still felt that he was betraying her as he took picture after picture.

It was possible that someone in the police department was involved and had revealed her location, so it only made sense to make sure there were copies available in case they "disappeared" while in the evidence locker. And the revelation that there was something concrete that Alana's father had hidden, and that her mother had relocated, indicated there *was* evidence in existence that could shed light on what had happened twenty-five years ago. Evidence that might still bring someone to justice, someone who'd gotten away with possible murder all that time ago. The stakes were high, and he couldn't compromise them by indulging in finer feelings and worrying that Alana might see this as a betrayal.

Sweat trickled down his back, despite the cool temperature in the house. He managed to take copies of every piece of paper and upload it to the cloud, carefully returning everything to the order Alana had left them in. Then he deleted everything from his phone. By the time she came back to the kitchen, he was standing at the door, ready to escort her to the police station.

"We have a problem," Alana said, and he stilled. Had she stepped out of her room while the shower was running, seen him taking photos of her papers? Was she going to yell at him, call for help, kick him out?

"What problem?" He kept his voice level, but he was braced for whatever she might do.

"You're supposed to pick up Rex before the clinic closes. He needs to be watched, but he doesn't need a vet, and I don't want to stay at the clinic overnight with him again if I don't have to."

He couldn't blame Alana for not wanting another night in the clinic. Caleb didn't want that, either. But Rex was his responsibility, so he needed to get his dog.

"We can stop there after we go to the police station."

Alana frowned. Had he overstepped? Were they not going to the police station together?

"The clinic is closing soon, and I might be held up at the police station."

There would be a lot of questions for her. "I'm not letting you go alone, not while you're carrying that—" he indicated the papers on the kitchen table "—and people might try again to abduct you."

Alana twisted her lips as she considered, gathering up the papers at the same time. "Honestly, I don't want to go on my own, either. But it's not fair to hold up my staff."

Alana's safety was a bigger priority, in his mind. But she had a compromise.

"Why don't we both drive? You can follow me to the police station, make sure I get there okay. I'll be safe once I'm inside and hand this over. Hopefully. You can go to the clinic and get Rex while I talk to the officers investigating what's been happening to me. Whether this is what they want or not, I'll be safe while I'm at the station."

"Once I pick up Rex, I'll come back to the station and check on you."

Alana shook her head. "You bring Rex home. I'll be fine—I can text you, so you know I'm okay."

He didn't like her suggestion, but he had the dog to consider. The dog who'd kept Alana safe. He owed Rex. Reluctantly he agreed. Alana had brought out a plastic folder, carefully sealed all the documents inside and dropped it in a bag. She picked up her purse and waited for him to exit before her.

He pulled out his own keys and fiddled with them while Alana set the alarm and locked the door before looking up to smile at him. He smiled back, without thinking, and watched her cross to her car, chirping it open and sliding inside.

He jogged to his own vehicle to be ready to follow her to the police station. Follow closely. He would risk running a yellow light to make sure Alana stayed right in front of him.

His eyes were moving in every direction on the short trip: checking his rearview mirror for a tail, flicking from side to side for anyone trying to cut in, looking ahead to make sure Alana was safe in front of him. It was a relief when she pulled into a parking space in front of the station.

He stopped, blinkers on, to wait until she was safely inside.

The car door opened, and Alana stepped out. She bent over to pick up her purse and the bag with the documents, and straightened. Caleb checked the sidewalk, making sure no one passing by was paying attention to her.

The sound of a wound-up engine roared past him. A motorcycle, rider hunched over the handlebars, squealed brakes as it neared Alana, and then a gloved hand grabbed her purse and the bag. He dropped a foot to the ground, supporting the bike while he and Alana tugged for a moment, before the rider won the battle and sped off. Alana tried to hang on to her possessions, but the final pull from the motorcyclist knocked her to the ground. Caleb, already out of his SUV, had to choose between following the fleeing vehicle and checking on Alana.

Alana pushed herself up onto her knees as he dropped beside her.

"Are you hurt?" He held out a hand, ready to offer support if she needed it.

Her eyes were wide-open, her face pale. "He just… he just grabbed—and now it's gone."

Her lip was quivering. She'd had so much to deal with over the past day. The past couple of weeks.

"I'm so sorry. Are you hurt?"

She shook her head. Her jeans were dusty and her palms scraped, but he couldn't see any other indication of harm. He was tempted to run his hands over her, make sure she was uninjured, but he didn't have that right.

"Can you stand up? We should report this."

Alana took in a long breath, and then nodded. Caleb helped her to her feet.

"You're sure you're okay?"

Alana brushed her jeans. She swung her head around, checking for another attack. "Physically I'm fine. But… the papers are gone." Caleb heard shock and pain in her voice. He hadn't kept her safe.

She wasn't blaming him, but thinking about her loss. Whoever was after the papers, they had them now. Thank goodness he'd taken photos. Dare he tell her that?

Alana straightened her shoulders. "I'm angry. Angry at myself for not being more careful, angry at whoever took the only thing I have from my father."

People had noticed what had happened, and an officer from the police station came up to them. "Is everyone okay? What happened here?"

Alana gave him a twisted smile. "I was coming to give something to you guys, when I was mugged. It has to do with the break-in at my house, and the attempted abduction yesterday."

This was a beat cop, young and inexperienced. His eyes opened wide, and he looked around as if he thought someone more senior would show up soon to assist him.

Caleb put a hand under Alana's elbow, offering support. "Let's go in and make a report."

It took a long time to give their statements and talk with the detectives in charge of the case. Caleb wasn't familiar with this side of the process. If he gave them his RCMP credentials, things would go more quickly, at least for him, but he wasn't supposed to do that. Neither could he tell them that he had taken photos of the documents in question. When this was all done, though, case settled and Alana safe, he would share those with Alana. She deserved to have some record of what her father had written.

Alana called her staff and asked one of them to watch Rex until she and Caleb were done. The door of her vehicle had been damaged in the attack: the driver's side wouldn't close properly. The police were keeping it temporarily, so Caleb, whose SUV had been parked by another officer, offered to take the two of them home when they were done.

They went by the vet clinic to pick up Rex. Alana thanked her assistant for staying, and Caleb carefully carried the dog out to the back of the SUV. Rex appeared happier to see Alana than Caleb, which Caleb understood. He'd asked Yoxall to find more information about Rex when he'd sent the photos, and maybe if he had that, he could get closer to the dog. For now, Alana made sure he was settled, and Rex appreciated her care.

"Should we grab some takeout?" They'd missed dinner.

Alana nodded, and then frowned. There were shadows forming under her eyes, and her shoulders sagged. "I don't have any money. The motorcycle driver took my purse. I don't have my wallet, my phone, my ID, my bank card…even my passport."

"I'll pay for dinner. Not a problem, and if you need to, you can pay me back once you get things worked out. Make a list of what was stolen. Cancel your cards, and then reach out to get more ID in the morning."

Alana shoved her long brown hair, free of its usual ponytail, back with one hand. "This is going to be a hassle."

"You're right. It is. Do you have copies of your documents?"

She nodded. "Yeah. Scanned everything when I got it. Okay, that's tomorrow's problem. I'd appreciate it if you would pay for dinner, and I'll owe you."

Caleb planned to expense the meal, but he could tell her later. "I'm the newbie here. Where should we go? It'll have to be takeout since we've got Rex with us."

The ensuing discussion of the best burgers and shawarma in the neighborhood brought some sparkle back to Alana's eyes, and they stopped at the place she swore had the best shawarma in the city. Alana stayed in the car with Rex, doors locked, while Caleb picked up their order from the restaurant. Alana probably was safe, but he wasn't taking any chances.

"Do you want to come into my place to eat? I've kept you so busy I know you haven't had a chance to get settled in. I can give Rex another check-over, too." Caleb examined her expression and was reassured that she did want his—their—company. With all that had gone on, she might not want to be alone. He didn't want to leave her on her own, either.

Alana carried the food into the house while Caleb brought the dog. She fussed over Rex while Caleb laid out their selections. Rex lay with his head up and pulled himself to a sitting position.

"He's going to be fine," Alana promised, a hand smoothing the dog's head.

"I think he's grateful to you," Caleb teased.

She shrugged and crossed to join him at the table. "I'm not always popular with my clients. I have to hurt them or make them uncomfortable sometimes to make them better."

Like Caleb was doing now. Alana would be hurt when she found out why he was here, but it was for her benefit, long term. He kept reminding himself of that.

Over their food, they didn't mention any of the events of the past day. Alana shared information about Winnipeg, things that Caleb might like to do while he was here. Caleb in return described what it had been like growing up in Toronto—largest city in the country, but each section of the city with its own identity. They shared interests and favorite foods.

It was like a nice, getting-to-know-you date. Caleb hated that this woman he was drawn to was off-limits until the assignment was over, and then he'd probably never see her again. They'd go their separate ways: Alana would stay here, and Caleb finally would get to do the undercover work he and his father had been dreaming of. Of course he'd found someone he was interested in, when he was no longer able to be involved.

Once they'd finished their food, Alana suggested

he check on Rex while she took care of the few dishes they'd dirtied. Caleb would have offered to clean up instead, but he didn't know where things belonged, and he needed to connect with Rex. He hadn't yet checked on how Rex's owner was doing, or how to get more information on how to handle the dog from him.

He crossed the room and knelt by the dozing Rex. Rex's eyes opened, and Caleb swore he heard the dog asking what he wanted. He held out a hand to Rex's nose. Dogs were big on scents, right?

Rex's nose twitched and he lifted his head. Caleb twisted to check on the bandages wrapped on Rex's side. Alana had mentioned putting a cone around the dog's neck to prevent him from disturbing them if necessary. Rex hadn't bothered them yet.

"You're doing good, Rex."

Could a dog raise his eyebrows? It looked like he had.

"Yeah, I don't know dogs. But I appreciate you doing this for me, and what you did to protect Alana. I know you'd rather stay with her, and I don't blame you, but I'll do the best I can."

Rex lowered his head again. Caleb wasn't sure if that was resignation, or despair. Since his hand was there, he patted the top of Rex's head. Rex sighed.

Alana finished in the kitchen and moved into the living room with them. The long summer prairie evenings meant there was still plenty of daylight to see by.

"You know, I don't mind if you leave Rex here. I'm happy to check on him."

She knelt by the dog and scratched her hands over his neck and shoulder. Rex pressed against her, enjoying the movement. Her hands were trembling. He didn't think that was for Rex.

"Would you prefer to keep Rex here so he can give you some warning if anyone comes around?"

Alana's hands stilled, and her gaze flew up to his face. "Oh, I—" Her cheeks flushed.

"Hey, you've had a rough day. A rough couple of days—weeks. People not only attacked you, they've broken into your house, your safe place. It's normal for you to feel nervous."

She shook her head. "It's silly. I mean, they took the papers, and they've already searched the house for anything else they wanted. They're probably long gone, doing whatever with them."

Her voice expressed her frustration. He was tempted to tell her about his photos, again, but then he'd have to explain why he'd done it.

"We don't know for sure it was the same people, or that those papers were what they were looking for. I'd be nervous, too."

Her brows rose. "Really?"

He considered. Home broken into, attempted abduction, theft—and on top of all that, the shock of finding out you weren't who you thought you were, and your parent had lied to you for almost all your life.

He nodded. "I'd be upset. And want my gun nearby."

A corner of her mouth quirked up. "I'm upset, but I don't have a gun."

He almost offered to lend her his. He couldn't do that. But maybe...

"If you'd feel better, I could stay. Sleep on the couch here, keep an eye on Rex."

Her eyes widened. "Oh, I couldn't ask you to do that."

She was worried about his comfort, not saying that she didn't want him to stay. He shrugged. "You didn't. I offered. It's not a bad idea, really. You might feel safer with someone in the house, and I have a vet on call if anything happens to Rex."

Rex exhaled, and it sounded suspiciously close to a snort.

Alana looked at Rex and back to him. She'd only known him for a little over twenty-four hours. Of course she didn't want him to sleep on her couch.

"Sorry, I get it. Bad idea. You hardly know me—"

Alana shook her head. "No, it's not that. I spent last night with you at the clinic, didn't I? It's just that this won't be comfortable for you, and I need to learn to handle being here on my own."

Caleb liked this idea the longer he considered it, so he pushed. Whoever was after Alana was upping the stakes. If it was the Fowlers, they had motivation, resources and possibly desperation. Sleeping on the couch beat his intention of watching the house from the apartment over the garage all night. "That's true, but like you said, it's been a lot. If you need some time to get back to normal, that's understandable. I wouldn't have offered if I hadn't been willing. If it would make you feel better, I'll bunk here for the night. I'll just go to the apartment and grab a toothbrush."

Alana turned to the dog. "What do you think, Rex? Are you happy to stay here tonight?"

The dog licked her hand. Caleb agreed with him. Staying with Alana was no hardship.

Alana rose to her feet. "Part of me says that I haven't known you long, and I shouldn't take advantage of you like this. But another part of me wonders if God sent you to help get me through this."

The guilt hit Caleb again. She didn't know his real reason for being here. But maybe she was right. Maybe God was behind all of this.

Chapter Eight

Alana heard Caleb settling in on the couch. It was comfortable as far as couches went, and she'd given him a couple of pillows and a quilt, but it was still a couch. She'd offered him her spare room, but he wanted to be near Rex, and near the door, just in case. Everything grew quiet in the living room, and she tried to relax into sleep.

She couldn't turn off her brain. Her body was tired, but there was too much to think about. One big problem was the identification that had been stolen with her purse. She'd canceled her cards and made a list of what she needed to request replacements for. That was going to be a hassle.

Would those be flagged because of the change in her name? She couldn't remember having any problems when she first got her driver's license and passport, but had her mother intervened?

There was the whole issue of someone breaking into her home, attempting to abduct her then stealing her things. It was possible that the guy on the motorcycle wasn't actually after those documents and it had been a coincidence, but too much was happening too fast to really believe that. She hadn't been able to think of anything else someone might want from her.

She was grateful to Caleb for staying with her.

She could put all those problems aside, leave them in God's hands, but she couldn't let go of the fact that she wasn't who she'd thought she was.

Why had her mother never told her? Had she not trusted Alana? When she was a child she might have blurted out a truth by accident, but she was in her twenties now, and more than capable of keeping a secret.

What had her father been like, and was she like him? Who would she have been, and what would her life have been like, if she and her mother hadn't come to Winnipeg? If her father had kept on the right side of the law, and they'd remained a family together in Toronto?

Did she really know her mother? Apparently not.

It had always been the two of them. Her mother had never dated, said she'd never gotten over Alana's father. Amanda's father. The man had been alive, so that explained why her mother hadn't been interested in dating again.

Did her mother think Alana would have judged her for the man she'd married and had a child with? Had she ever had siblings? Were the documents from the safety deposit box even real? Was this some kind of hoax? Was there anyone in Winnipeg who knew the truth? What was the truth?

She had so many questions, and no one to ask.

She tried to pray about it, but she didn't find the calm she was used to. When she couldn't trust the woman who raised her, it was more difficult to trust her heavenly Father. If her mother had been dishonest, and God had allowed it… She didn't know much about witness protection, despite having been involved with it for most of her life. Someone here must have known, been keeping an eye on them. Right? Or were people in witness protection just left, abandoned?

Mr. Conners? Someone else in the police department? Her pastor, her neighbors—she couldn't trust anyone. Could someone she knew be involved in this past crime? Unless maybe it was all a hoax—but why?

She rolled over in bed, again, her mind still racing. She was even more grateful for Caleb. She could trust him— he wasn't part of this. He'd shown up after it all began. He wasn't a cop, wasn't someone who could have been part of the new identities set up for her mother and herself.

Her mind returned to her mother. She remembered, when she was smaller and had asked about her father, that her mother would sometimes tell her stories. Stories about how he'd played with her as an infant, how he loved her, how he and her mother had met. She didn't know if any of those stories were real.

She finally dozed off, dreaming in a half-awake state of her mother telling her stories and making them more and more incredible as she lost consciousness.

When she woke in the morning, her phone alarm beside her bringing her awake, she still felt tired and disoriented. But her subconscious had been active while she slept. She had a plan, and she was going to do something to find out what her past was, and who her parents really were. And maybe figure out the mystery of why someone was after her as well.

When she'd readied herself and made her way to the kitchen, she found Caleb ahead of her. He'd dressed, and the bedding she'd given him to sleep on was folded on the end of the couch. He was kneeling by Rex, appearing to be in a conversation with the dog.

She'd sensed he wasn't comfortable with the animal, and it was good to see the two of them building a connection. Rex was a great dog. He'd been highly trained, based on the way he'd gone for her would-be abductor the other day, and would need his owner to be a leader. She should check her contacts to find someone to help Caleb understand what commands Rex was used to.

When Caleb heard her, he rose to his feet. "Good morning."

It was nice, having someone there in the house with her again. "Good morning. Were you able to get any sleep on the couch?"

He smiled at her, and she felt that. "I did, believe it or not. Think I was pretty tired. Rex didn't move all night as far as I can tell, so I was just thanking him."

Alana moved over to examine the dog. He'd left his bandages undisturbed, and when she checked, the wound was healing well. She rubbed his head, and his tail thumped the floor. "You're an excellent patient, Rex. Think you're ready to try the outdoors?"

"Is that wise?" Caleb asked.

She helped Rex get to his feet. "We have an enclosed backyard—from our previous dog. I think getting outside will be good for him."

Rex followed her to the kitchen, and she opened the back door. There were only two steps to the yard, and Rex handled them safely. He sniffed at some bushes and lifted his leg in the back corner.

Caleb was watching from behind her. She looked back and up at him. "Our dog always peed there as well."

He grinned. "It must be a dog thing. Why don't you go back in and I'll wait for Rex to finish up."

Alana left Caleb to deal with Rex and turned to the coffee maker, using the busy work to settle herself again. By the time Caleb had helped Rex in, and refilled his food and water, Alana had the coffee almost done.

"What do you put in your coffee? Or do you not drink it?"

Caleb gave her another smile. "I may not actually drink it—first thing in the morning I inhale it."

Alana laughed and filled a mug, handing it to Caleb. "I have milk, creamer—hazelnut flavor—and sugar?"

"Creamer and sugar if you don't mind."

Alana opened a cupboard, relieved to find there was sugar in the sugar bowl, and it wasn't rock-hard yet. She used the creamer for her own coffee but passed on the sugar. Her mother had— She shut that thought off. She pulled a spoon out of a drawer so Caleb could stir and leaned against the kitchen counter with her cup.

"You ever go to bed with a problem bothering you, and then wake up in the morning with a solution your brain worked on overnight?"

Caleb nodded. "Are you saying you thought of something?" He leaned forward slightly, as if eager to hear.

"It took me some time to fall asleep. I was tired, but still pretty wired. And we don't know for sure, but I think this other story of my life, before we came to Winnipeg, that must be what all these attacks are about, right?"

Caleb nodded.

"Because there's been nothing that would inspire that since. I've been wracking my brain for a week and couldn't think of anything. This is the only thing that's logical. But I'm not sure those papers are what they were really after."

Caleb set down his mug. "No?"

Alana shook her head. "I know they were stolen, but I did read everything, and unless my dad was using some kind of code, there was nothing in those letters that anyone would need to do all this for."

"That's a good point." Caleb had his head tilted, listening.

"But the letter my mom wrote him, and never sent. She mentioned moving something. And that something might be what all this is about."

"I'm following you." Caleb stopped after that, letting her continue.

"Unless that's in code, too, and if so, I can't do anything about it. The only person who knows where this missing thing is was my mom and she didn't tell anyone, as far as we know."

"So it's lost forever, and maybe people will leave you alone?"

She couldn't pinpoint the tone or expression on his face, but something made her think he didn't really believe that. She didn't think so, either. These people, whoever they were, might believe her mother had told her about this. Maybe that it was hidden in this house, and they might return to look for it.

They might tear the house apart. And pressure her to reveal a hiding place she had no knowledge of. Her alarm gave her some safety, and Caleb more, but if someone was determined...

"I have no idea how far these people will go, because I have no idea what this thing is. But I may know where it is."

Caleb's eyes blazed. "Really? Did she have a favorite hiding place, somewhere she'd keep things safe that she wouldn't leave at the bank?"

Alana shook her head slowly. "No, not that she shared. After her first stroke, her memory and speech were greatly compromised. It was almost impossible to understand anything she tried to say, if she'd wanted to tell me something, and she didn't have the muscle control to write. Before then, she didn't tell me anything about our past, let alone a secret hiding place. But she did, sometimes, more often when I was small, tell me stories about my dad."

She needed another cup of coffee and moved over to the pot. Caleb was leaning beside it, and his knuckles on the countertop were white. He was worried—about her? She looked up. Their eyes met, and for a moment, she forgot the problems she had to deal with. She stared into his eyes and shivered as he stared back. Caleb looked away.

Alana wasn't sure how to handle that moment. She'd been drawn in, attracted and comforted. But she didn't know Caleb, not well. It had only been a couple of days. And she had bigger problems to deal with. What had she been saying? Right. Her mother and stories about her dad.

"I think I know where they had their last date together. Same place as their first date. I'm going to go there and see if anything is hidden."

Caleb stood upright. "Alana—that could be dangerous. They could follow you. You shouldn't do something like that alone. Would it be okay if I came with you, made sure you're safe?"

The idea of having someone with her, someone to

help protect her was appealing. But could she really ask that of Caleb? She didn't know what she'd find, nor were they close. Could she trust him?

There was another problem. "You need to take care of Rex."

"Could we take him to your clinic? Pay someone there to keep an eye on him for a couple of hours while we check this out?"

Alana shook her head. "No. Because my father was never in Winnipeg, or anywhere on the prairies as far as I know. My dad was born and raised in Toronto, but my mom grew up in Barrie, just north of there. I'm going to fly to Toronto and rent a car to get to Barrie. That's where they had their last date."

Chapter Nine

No. Absolutely not. Alana could not travel to Toronto, not on her own, and do anything so dangerous as try to find what her mother had hidden.

If the evidence from the jewelry store altercation existed, someone was desperate to find it. If it proved the presence of the second cop that his father and Yoxall suspected, Robert Fowler, he was a man with skills and access to a wide range of resources through his father. The attempted abduction demonstrated that. Alana might not know what Fowler needed to know, but he could do a lot of harm to her before he believed she was ignorant.

He opened his mouth to tell her no and stopped. For the first time since she'd discovered her past, she looked energized. He had to discourage her from doing it, though. If he couldn't as Caleb Johnson, he might have to break his cover.

"I'm not sure that's a good idea." He threw that out for starters.

"Why not?" She had her hands on her hips, determination written on her face.

"Because—" He tried to think of a good reason. "You don't have your identification. You'll need a passport to fly."

It took a while to get a replacement passport.

"I can get a replacement driver's license today."

"Do the replacements have a photo?"

Alana's face fell. "I don't know. And my car isn't drivable, and I don't know if I can rent one with a replacement license, and I don't have a credit card. I'll have to take the bus or train."

With the risk that whoever was after her got on the bus or train as well? Not happening.

"Maybe you should tell someone else where you think this thing is hidden, and they can take care of it for you. It's a long trip, and you have work."

With her arms crossed, she furrowed her brows as she stared at the floor. "You think I should tell the police?"

Oh, no. Especially not the police in Ontario. If Yoxall was right, that was asking for Fowler Senior to track down and find the evidence. Fowler had worked for the Toronto police, and his father had high-up connections in the Ontario Provincial Police. Between them, there was a good chance the evidence would disappear. Would Alana be collateral damage, now that she was putting together the pieces?

"I'm not sure if that would keep you safe." He was hedging while his mind raced.

"You think I might still be at risk? They might come after me?"

He did but couldn't tell her why. "Since we don't know what we're dealing with, yes."

She sighed. "I don't know what I'd tell the police. *Officer, the papers I planned to give the police here in*

Winnipeg dropped a hint about something my mother hid, which might be important since my house was broken into. I don't know what it is, or why someone would want it, but maybe you could look around for it for me?"

That was his opening. "Do you know where it is? So that someone could easily find it?"

"I do, and I don't. I mean, I know within probably the distance of a city block, but not more detailed than that. And it's a long shot, based on a story my mother told me that I'm not even sure is true. This is so frustrating!"

She hadn't named the place. Did she not want to tell him? Did she not trust him?

He glanced at his phone. She needed to go to work. He hoped she wouldn't get any more ideas about traveling east, but maybe he could offer again to go with her, so that he knew what she was doing. And where and when.

"Do you have to go into the clinic today?"

She shot a glance at the clock on the microwave. "Yes! I have to get moving, or I'll be late."

"Then Rex and I should get out of your way."

Alana glanced from him to the dog. "I'm sorry— you haven't been able to get any of your own work done since you've been here. I've tied up all your time."

"I don't mind, Alana, really. My stuff—it's something that happened years ago, and nothing I write about is going to make much difference to anyone."

"That's not always true. Whatever my problem is also happened years ago, and it's making a difference to you and me."

He nodded. "True. And just so you know, if you do decide to go east, I would go with you."

She stilled. Had he overstepped? He tried to downplay it. "You've got me a little curious, and I am worried about you."

She was frowning. "That's a generous offer."

"I'm serious. I'd worry about you while you were gone anyway."

Her expression softened, and he thought he had her.

"You have Rex to take care of, though."

They both looked at the dog, curled up on a blanket. He was improving, but he wasn't back to his normal physical condition.

Caleb wasn't giving up. "We could bring Rex with us. Take my rental SUV, Rex in the back. He's supposed to rest anyway, right? He can rest while we drive, and we can stop anytime we need to for him. And that takes care of your ID problem."

Alana looked from him to the dog. "Thank you. I appreciate your offer, but that's too much to ask."

It wasn't really. It would give him the perfect opportunity to do his job. And he'd feel much better knowing someone was looking out for Alana. If he pushed, though, she'd get suspicious.

He'd talk to Yoxall. See if they'd gotten anywhere looking for codes in the letters Alana's mother and father had written. If he could get Alana to tell him where she thought this hidden stash was, he could make sure someone was protecting her, even if it wasn't him.

Meanwhile, he'd drive her to work and back, since her car was still at the police lot.

Alana protested when he insisted on driving her to the clinic, but since she didn't have a car, she needed a ride. Caleb made sure she got safely in the door of the clinic, and she promised him that while she was working she'd take all necessary precautions in case someone was still looking for her.

Caleb had boosted Rex into the back of the SUV to take Alana to the clinic. Now, back in the driveway he and Alana shared, he opened the hatch to find Rex waiting for him.

He wasn't afraid Rex would leap out, not now that he'd spent time with the dog, and not with his injury. He tried to think like a dog owner.

"Do you need to pee on a bush before we go inside?"

Rex didn't react.

"Let's give it a try. I've got a lot of calls to make once we get upstairs."

He helped Rex to the ground, and the dog made his own way to a hedge and lifted his leg. Then he followed Caleb to the steps and allowed Caleb to carry him upstairs. Carrying Rex was a workout, but Caleb would need to do more than that to keep in shape. He hadn't set up a routine yet. Another thing to add to his to-do list.

He hadn't spent any length of time in the apartment yet. His duffel bag was on the bed, opened where he'd rifled through to find clothes. Rex's stuff—food, bowls and other things Caleb needed to check out—was in a bag on the table. Rex was looking at it with a laser focus, so Caleb made sure the dog had food and water and his bed set up before he took a shower.

When he came out, Rex's food bowl was empty, and the dog was curled up on his bed. Good, he could concentrate on work now. He was getting the hang of dog ownership.

He sat on the couch and called Yoxall. The familiar, gruff voice greeted him.

"Caleb. How are things going?"

"It's been a pretty eventful couple of days."

He heard the other man snort. "Did you just stumble in at the right time, or are you the cause?"

Caleb rolled his eyes, grateful that they weren't on video. "Just stumbled, I guess. Have you found anything in those letters?"

"No. My code guy has had to look at them on the down-low, since this isn't official and we don't want anyone to know what we're doing, but he doesn't see anything that looks like a code. The most interesting bit is in that letter of her mother's that says she moved whatever was hidden, but that doesn't help much. Doesn't say what she moved or where she moved it. Does indicate there might be something around."

Caleb settled in his seat. "That was one of the things I wanted to talk to you about. Alana thinks she may know the place her mother was talking about."

Now Yoxall's voice was excited. "Did she tell you where it is? I can get someone there immediately."

"She gave some hints, but not the exact place."

"Hints?"

Caleb took a look at the notes he'd scribbled down on a pad of paper before he called.

"She's basing her idea on stories her mother told her about her dad, before he supposedly died. She's not sure if those stories are true, but she wants to go and check out the place her mother talked about, where they had their last date."

"They were in Ontario then."

"I know. She wanted to fly out to Toronto this weekend, but she doesn't have a passport. Or any identification, since her purse was stolen. She's getting a temporary driver's license, but it doesn't have a photo."

"If she'll tell you where it is, we can do that for her."

"I pushed, just a bit, but she wouldn't say, except that it was back in Ontario where her mother grew up, and that she could only nail down an area about a city block in size."

Yoxall sighed gustily over the line. "That doesn't help much."

"If I keep pressing her, I think she'll spook and shut me out. Unless I tell her who I really am, then she'd probably share whatever information she has."

She'd also be upset with Caleb. She'd been open with him, and he'd been playing a role.

Or had he? Other than not telling her who he was, he hadn't been pretending. His urge to protect her was more than his job. But he had information he'd kept from her: he knew what had happened with her father and mother all those years ago. Information that would help her process and understand what was going on. He'd like to be able to share that with her. He'd like to start being honest.

Yoxall interrupted his thoughts. "Don't say anything just yet. If she can't fly, and her car is still being checked over, she can't take off without you knowing, correct?"

"Correct." He'd make sure she didn't go anywhere without him knowing. And following, if he wasn't with her.

"Keep your cover as long as you can. We may need it." So, being honest with her was out.

"I offered to drive her to Ontario."

"Good work. That could be perfect. We can track you, find a way to provide backup if you need it."

Maybe he should try to do that with Alana's phone. Set it up so he could follow it. His shoulders slumped. It had been in her purse when her things were stolen, so she had no phone. What if the thieves were accessing it? What could they do? He hated the idea that they could spy on her with the device.

Or…and this was a disturbing thought, maybe they'd put something in the house when they'd broken in. Then they would have known Alana had gone to the bank and found the contents of the safety deposit box. They would have known when he and Alana were heading to the police station with those contents and had the motorcyclist set up ready to steal her purse when she got there.

"Is there any chance that Alana's place is bugged? These people broke in twice—maybe once was to set up a bug. They've been listening in, and that's how they knew to intercept us before we got to the station with her mother's papers?"

Yoxall was silent for a moment. "I didn't consider that. Didn't want to spook Alana or anyone else by paying too much attention to what was happening there. But if this is big enough and important enough… I hate the idea that a dirty cop has got away with theft, and possibly murder. And that one might get elected."

If someone had been listening, they would have heard that Alana thought she knew where her mother had hidden this thing, probably the evidence.

"If Alana decides to hop the train to head east, they could know about that. Maybe I have to tell her what's going on so we can look around."

"Don't be too hasty. Let me see what I can do. I have some people I can reach out to, check on what's in her house without giving alarm. I'll be back to you—stay put for now."

Yoxall hung up, leaving Caleb frustrated. His mind spiraled down different paths, considering possibilities and ramifications. He'd never contacted Yoxall from Alana's house, but if there was a device in this apartment, then the people involved would know who he really was.

They hadn't paid any attention to him so far. And this place hadn't been broken into. Maybe his cover was still good.

Still, even if they'd only put a device in Alana's house, they'd know everything that Alana knew. Now he was grateful she hadn't told him more details about where her mother might have hidden something. He'd have to ensure that they didn't say anything of importance while in her house. Unless he was there all the time, though, what was to stop her talking to someone else?

Would the clinic be safe? There were people in and out of it all day, so installing a device might not be difficult. Could they be listening there? Would Alana talk about this to anyone at her work?

"What do we do, Rex?"

Rex lifted his head at the sound of his name but had no answers.

Chapter Ten

Alana got a message from her receptionist, between appointments, that the police wanted her to call. If she was lucky, she might be able to get her car back and the door fixed. Something was urging her to go to Ontario. This was a chance to explore her roots. Maybe learn about the years before she and her mother moved to Winnipeg. Discover what her father—the real man, not the one her mother had curated for her—was like.

It was more than curiosity, though. She couldn't feel safe while there was something out there, possibly hidden by her mother, that people were willing to harm her for. Rather than wait on another attempt, she wanted to be proactive. Maybe finding this would enable her to return to the safe life she'd thought she had.

She called and was put through to one of the detectives.

"We want to take another look at your house." He didn't waste time on small talk.

"You want to look at my house?" Why? Everything was cleaned up from the break-ins, and anything of in-

terest had been stolen from her by the man on the motorcycle.

"We need to go inside, check a couple of things."

Her receptionist signaled that her next patient was
waiting. She didn't understand and didn't have time to
go into details. But maybe...

"I'll contact my tenant, ask him to let you in." And
keep an eye on whatever was going on.

"Sure. Is your tenant on the premises?"

"I believe so—he should be in the apartment over
the garage."

"Good. We're heading over, will let you know if
there's a problem."

"Thank you."

Alana hung up, held up a finger to her impatient
receptionist, and quickly texted Caleb on the cheap
burner phone she'd asked Mauve to pick up for her.
One with a different phone number, so it couldn't be
traced to her.

This is Alana. Police want to look in the house again,
for some reason. Can you let them in and keep an
eye on them?

Alana was suspicious of everyone right now.

Happy to. Got a replacement phone?

It was a relief to know there was another set of eyes
looking out for trouble.

Yes to the phone. Spare set of keys in cutlery drawer
in UR place. Will text alarm code separately.

Caleb responded immediately again.

Let U know what happens.

With that, Alana found she could push the matter to the back of her mind and concentrate on Trickie's ear infection.

She didn't hear back from the police or Caleb before she finished her workday. When she came out after her last patient, Caleb was in the waiting room with Rex. He'd promised to give her a ride home, but the expression on his face indicated that something was up.

"Is anything wrong?"

He held a finger to his mouth, and then smiled. "No, just here to give you a lift back. Any word on your car yet?"

Alana narrowed her eyes. If he'd been with the police, he'd know she hadn't heard anything further. He shook his head, the slightest amount to the side. Whatever was up he didn't want her to mention it.

"No, I haven't heard about my car. I'll be another fifteen minutes."

"No problem. Take your time."

He settled into a seat. Rex lay down at his feet. She blew out a frustrated sigh and turned back to finish her notes.

When she came out again, she'd changed out of her scrubs into regular clothes. She didn't know what was going on, but she wanted to be prepared.

Caleb and Rex stood and went through the front doors. Alana's receptionist and assistant had already left through the back, and she'd locked up behind them. She finished setting the alarm before locking the front door.

Caleb stood beside her, eyes scanning the parking lot.

"What's going on?"

"We can talk in the car." Caleb popped the button on his fob to open up the hatch, and Alana followed him. She might as well check out how Rex was doing.

Caleb lifted him up, but Rex was almost ready to jump on his own. The bandages were clean, with no staining. It would take a while for the scars to heal and the hair to regrow, but Rex was nearly ready to assume his usual activity.

"He's good?" Caleb had watched her examination closely.

"*He* is."

Caleb jerked his head toward the vehicle door, and Alana got in. Once Caleb had slammed the hatch down, he got in his own side and put the vehicle in gear.

"They found a bug in your house." Caleb pulled the car out into traffic, while Alana considered his words.

"You don't mean an insect."

He shook his head. "A listening device. Just one. It was in the kitchen."

Alana shuddered. Someone had been listening to her? At least it wasn't the bedroom or bathroom. She tried to remember anything that she and Caleb had discussed in the kitchen. The bug had to be related to the break-ins. Her life had been boring prior to this. The life she'd thought she had. There might have been a lot of excitement before she changed from Amanda to Alana.

Focusing on the past few days, Alana remembered

going through the paperwork from the safety deposit box at the kitchen table. They'd discussed going to the police...

"That's how they knew I was going to the police with all those documents."

Caleb nodded.

"Is it gone?" Was there any reason they might have considered it worth leaving it in her kitchen?

"Yes. They're going to try to track down where it came from and who would have put it there, but it's something you can buy online."

That meant they'd probably never find out where it came from.

"Whoever was listening would have heard that I don't have any copies, right? They have no reason to bother me anymore."

"They also could have heard you tell me you thought you knew the hiding spot."

She slumped against her seat, then looked out the window. Caleb was driving around her neighborhood and must have passed her house a few blocks ago.

"Where are you going?"

"I didn't know if you wanted to go to your home right away."

She didn't. The bug might be gone, but the sense of violation lingered.

"You're right. I need to think."

"Maybe we can pick up some takeout again, go to a park or something. You can think out loud if you want and no one will be listening in."

That sounded good. And it would be good to have Caleb and Rex there. They made her feel safe. Safety was a feeling someone had taken away from her, with the break-ins and attempted abduction and mugging. Her fists clenched as she prayed for calm.

Once they'd picked up sub sandwiches and Alana directed them to a nearby park, they found an empty bench. Rex sat between their legs, watching everything happening in the park. Caleb had carried the food and passed Alana her sandwich and drink. She dropped her head for a moment to thank God for the food and ask for guidance.

She ate half her sandwich in silence, Caleb giving her the time to process. She appreciated that.

She set down the other half on the wrapper. "I'm in trouble."

"You are. But Rex and I will help all we can."

Alana examined the man beside her. Yes, he was attractive, and looked strong and fit enough to protect her physically. She'd initially trusted him because Mr. Conners had vouched for him.

But throughout these past few days, when things barreled at her without a break, he'd been a steady and supporting presence. If he'd had any designs on the things that had been in her mother's keeping, he could have made off with the letters easily. He hadn't. Instead, he'd protected her. Without him and Rex, she'd have been abducted.

If God brought someone into her life to help her when she needed it, she should take advantage.

"Whoever is doing this, they have the letters and all my identification, and they *know* that I might know where something is hidden."

Caleb nodded and waited while she worked it out.

"I need to find out what happened with my father, if there was anything not mentioned in the newspaper reports, and I need to find whatever my mother hid. Once that is given to the proper authorities, I'm no longer of any value to them, am I?"

Caleb studied her, his expression serious. "We can look up your father online—you have his name, and your mother's. There should be something there. But you don't need to find whatever your mother hid on your own. If we let someone know, someone in law enforcement, they can look for it instead."

Alana considered. "Two problems. Whoever thinks I have that information won't know that I've shared it, so they'll still be looking for me."

Caleb sighed. "Maybe we could get the police to put the bug back so you can tell them."

Alana frowned. "Would they not know that it was found by now—since there's no sounds or anything?"

"Possibly. What's the other problem?"

Alana made a frustrated gesture. "I can't tell anyone because I don't know exactly where I'm going."

Caleb's head tilted. "You said you knew where they had their date."

"I know what my mother said in her story, which I'm not sure is true. But she didn't give a definite location. It was at a drive-in movie theater near her hometown of Barrie. I don't know which one. I don't know if there are that many, and if they still exist.

"Even if I figure out which drive-in it is, and it's not been built over, a drive-in covers a lot of space, and she didn't mention a precise location."

Caleb's mouth quirked as he considered. "That is… daunting."

Alana stared at the baseball diamond at the back of the park but didn't see it. "I keep trying to pin down what exactly Mom said. But they were just stories. I'd ask her about my dad, what he was like, and she'd tell me stuff. But I don't even know if any of it is true."

Caleb picked up his wrapper. "I guess we should do some research on your father, find out if it matches what your mother told you, and then see if we can jump-start your memories."

Alana folded her sandwich up carefully. "Do you think it's safe to go back to the house?"

She hated that she didn't feel that her home, the place she'd grown up in and always found to be a safe retreat, was no longer that.

"Rex and I can stay with you again. The alarm will let us know if anyone breaks in, and it's one place we know now has no listening devices."

She almost cried with relief. But it was a big favor.

"I hate to ask you."

Caleb gave her a warm smile. "This is much more interesting than the research I was planning to do. And before you worry, no, I don't have a hard timeline, so I can take a break. I wouldn't be able to focus on hockey while I was worried about you anyway."

"This wasn't what you signed up for."

"There will be time for that. Let's go look up your family."

This was excruciating.

Alana had brought out her laptop to the kitchen table. Caleb could tell, from her frequent glances around, and the way she jerked when the fridge motor came on, that she was nervous and fearful. He wasn't leaving her on her own.

Rex made himself comfortable on the floor near

them. Having the alarm on was comforting, but Caleb knew Rex would hear intruders before there was a chance for the alarm to be triggered. As long as the dog was settled quietly at their feet, they were good.

On Caleb's laptop in the apartment was a file of Greg Campbell's history, crime, arrest and trial. Information that the police knew but hadn't shared. He couldn't reference any of that. Instead, he sat beside Alana as she entered the man's name in her browser window, and a bunch of other men with the same name but more recent history popped up. He had to hold his tongue while she clicked on articles that he knew were about someone else, and not guide her to the ones he knew were correct.

It was a relief when she finally had the right man, and the right story. Well, almost the right story. These were old newspaper articles, and the facts weren't always what the articles claimed. Some of the articles matched the clippings Alana's mother had kept, and some were more sensational.

He had to bite his tongue and let her figure out what was most likely the truth. He kept quiet because he wasn't sure how well he could coax her to the right conclusions without giving himself away. The articles disappeared after the sentencing, until a short piece gave notice of Greg Campbell's death.

Alana sat back. She'd scribbled down notes as she read through.

"My father was a jeweler, and he handled stolen goods."

Caleb made a sound of agreement. "That was in the clippings your mother had as well. He was convicted for that."

"My mother testified that he planned a theft to defraud his insurance company."

Caleb nodded. He wanted to comfort Alana because this was difficult for her to process, but he wasn't sure what she'd be willing to accept from him.

"That's why we were in witness protection. But if my father was in prison, what threat was there to us?"

Caleb pointed to a note she'd made. "The man who was killed, the one he was setting up the fake robbery with, was a cop."

Alana circled the note with her pen. "But he was dead. And that's terrible, and I feel bad for his family and friends, but would they have tried to hurt us, after my mother testified against my father?"

Caleb pointed to another note. "If there was someone else involved, a third party, maybe that third party was a danger." Only one place had referenced her mother's testimony about the third man.

Alana bit her lip. "True, but nothing came of that. It was just noted that one time, and there was no evidence."

"Nothing then, but what about now?"

Alana turned to him, eyes wide. "That third person could be whoever is after me. Who stole those papers. And my mother mentioned moving something—evidence?"

"That's an explanation for what's been going on with you."

Alana tapped the paper. "But if there were someone else, why wouldn't my father have said something? Why protect the man?"

"You and your mother."

"Okay, I can understand that. But that would mean

the third man had some power, or clout. Something to make a threat credible even if he was in prison himself. If Mom and I were being hidden in witness protection, then we should be safe."

There was a reason why that wouldn't work, and Caleb had to push Alana to that conclusion without tipping his hand. He let a moment pass, and then tapped the note on her pad.

"A policeman? You think the third person could be another police officer?"

Caleb liked that Alana found that idea difficult to grasp. Dirty cops were a black eye for the force and were more present than anyone liked.

"Just looking for reasons that would make sense."

Alana looked over her notes again. "So, my father went to prison for manslaughter and possession of stolen goods. The man who died was a cop. My mother and I went into witness protection, and if that was all there was to it, then what's been going on these past two weeks wouldn't be connected to what happened.

"But if there were a third person, someone my father was afraid of, then there may be evidence out there that would incriminate that third person, and it must be bad enough that the person is willing to break in, install a listening device, try to abduct me, and steal the papers I found even though they don't reveal anything."

"Right."

Her face twisted as she considered the information at her disposal. "If the thing Mom hid is that important, he's not going to stop until someone finds it. And I said I knew where it was."

"That makes me worried about your safety."

She tidied the papers together. "If that third person is a cop, then I can't really drop this on the lap of the police department. Unless there's some way to know who the possible third man is."

Caleb could tell her what the suspicions had been at the time, but only by revealing who he really was. And that only confirmed that telling the police would require choosing the right person.

Maybe it was worth it. Alana needed to be kept safe. But then, keeping her safe might mean that no one ever found out the real third man, or found enough evidence to implicate him. Which could endanger other people going forward.

He threw out a suggestion, just to see how she'd respond. "If you found and destroyed the evidence, and this possible third man knew, it would keep you safe."

Alana's eyes flashed. "I'm going to go with the hypothesis that the third man exists, and he's dangerous, whether a cop or not. There's some reason that he needs to protect himself, and he's willing to hurt others to do that. I'm not going to protect a dirty cop or criminal just to possibly keep myself safe. What's that quote—all that's needed for evil to prevail is for good people to do nothing?"

"Maybe he's not that evil."

"And maybe he is. I'm not the one to decide that."

Caleb put out a hand to hers, needing to reassure her. "I think you're doing the right thing, but you are in danger, if we're right. I'll stay on the couch again tonight. Which means Rex is here."

Alana nodded. "Thank you. I'm going to take you up on your offer—to drive me to Ontario. I'll arrange with the vet I took over from—get him to come out of retirement long enough to cover while we're gone. Then we're going on a road trip."

Chapter Eleven

Once Alana had made her calls and gone to her room for the night, Caleb texted Yoxall.

We're heading out for Ontario tomorrow morning. I'm driving Alana in my SUV.

Yoxall responded almost immediately.

What do you need?

Caleb appreciated the prompt response. He typed quickly:

Protection on the road. Can you handle that?

Since they'd found the bug in Alana's house, Caleb knew they were likely to be followed when they left.

What route are you taking?

We have to stay in Canada, which means we go over the Lakes—Alana has no ID.

Those roads are OPP territory, not RCMP. And you're going to lose cell coverage.

Caleb hadn't ever driven that route, but he wasn't surprised.

I can break my cover, maybe get an official escort.

Not sure that won't end up in the wrong ears. I'll reach out to some trusted guys, have them drive that route unofficially. I'll text you names once I've got it set up.

What about information on Rex?

Working on it.

Caleb considered his plan, such as it was. Alana remembered her parents having their last date at a drive-in but didn't know which one, or where it was, except that it was near where her mother had been raised in Barrie, Ontario. If she got to Barrie, she might be able to recognize something from her mother's stories, but it was a long shot. A long shot, but the only one they had.

If the third man from the crime was Fowler and he was after her, he would probably risk another abduction attempt to get that information from her. If Alana was alone— Caleb's blood chilled at the thought.

Better that she went with him. He could watch out for her. Maybe, once they got there, something would trigger a memory, and they could find this evidence.

More likely the drive-in was torn down or built over, but if it was still functioning, they could look around in the daytime when it wasn't open. If they didn't find anything, Caleb would have people he could call on to help. Yoxall, his father and some of his father's crew. Waiting here in Winnipeg indefinitely in a high state of risk wasn't a great idea.

Caleb and Rex were up first in the morning, and Caleb returned to his apartment with Rex, letting him water a bush before climbing to the apartment. The dog could climb the stairs on his own now. Caleb didn't have much to pack, since he'd barely unpacked. He ensured he had his pistol and ammunition ready. They'd be followed on this trip, if not intercepted. If Alana's abductor tried again and Caleb apprehended him, that might be enough to get cuffs on the guy. Then she would be free to search for this missing item without any danger. She could even have RCMP assistance, which would make things much easier.

Rex watched him with ears perked. Caleb grinned at him. "This familiar to you, buddy? Do you miss working?"

Rex whined. Caleb scratched behind his ears. "I know you're retired and injured, but you're coming with us. You have that nose and ears, much better than mine. You can let us know if someone's around who shouldn't be, and I can handle them this time. Deal?"

Rex lay down, sighing.

Caleb frowned. "Part of being a team is knowing each member's strengths and weaknesses. Let go of your ego and do what's best for the team. You're a dog, and yes, you're still pretty good, despite being retired. But I'm a cop, bud. I have a gun. I was ranked in the top ten for accuracy in our class shooting. I know how to take someone down."

He stopped because defending his abilities to the dog was an indication that something was wrong. Still. "You just wait, Rex. I'll show you."

Then, with the last of his clothes thrown in his duffel bag, he packed up food and treats for Rex. The dog watched with his muzzle resting on crossed forepaws.

"Right. We're a team. But I'm not the weakest link."

Alana had coffee ready in the kitchen when Caleb and Rex returned. The sun rose early, this far north, and it was full daylight despite the early hour.

She smiled at them. "Sleep well?"

Rex crossed to nose her hand. Caleb frowned at him. "Pretty good. You?"

She shrugged. "Took a while to get my brain shut off."

If only he could let her know there was going to be some covert protection for them. "You can sleep in the car."

She let out a frustrated sigh. "I want to do some of the driving. Be helpful."

"You're not on the rental agreement. Will they accept a temp license on that?"

Her face fell. "Probably not, but it's a long drive. You'll get tired and that will be dangerous."

"If you think I'm getting too tired, we'll stop. There are a couple of long stretches where there aren't motels, but other than that, we can take a break anytime we need to. We don't have a set schedule."

Alana shook her head. "We need to do this as quickly as possible."

He had that same anxious buzzing inside, but he was trying to be reasonable. "Understandable. But we're going to use our heads, not our anxiety, as a guideline. In any case, we have to make regular stops for Rex."

Alana squatted down to pet the dog. "I'm sorry, Rex, I was forgetting about you. You'll be happier if we make an overnight stop or two and regularly let you stretch your legs."

She stood up. "Okay if I check him again? He looks much better, but—"

Caleb nodded. She needed to feel useful and be busy. Once they started driving, she'd have nothing to do except check Rex when they made a stop. That and worry.

The coffee was good, and the caffeine woke up the corners of his brain that were still a little groggy. Alana had packed a cooler with drinks and sandwiches for their first day. After that, they'd buy their meals.

Caleb would do that. He'd taken out a large cash withdrawal so that Caleb Drekker's credit card didn't show activity in places he wasn't meant to be. Alana was waiting on a replacement bank card. That would be bothering her as well.

Twenty minutes later, after a quick breakfast and check around the house, they had the SUV packed up with a couple of duffel bags, the cooler, and the bag of food and supplies for Rex. Caleb helped Rex into the carrier in the back, and then it was time to go.

Once the seat belts were on, Alana asked, "Could we pray before we start?"

Caleb nodded. He had some names from Yoxall, guys he could trust who'd be on the road they were traveling the next couple of days, but he was happy to ask for protection from a higher power as well.

It was easy to forget this wasn't all on him.

Once they were on the Perimeter Highway, the bypass ringing the city of Winnipeg, they made good time. Then they shifted to the Trans-Canada Highway, which would take them almost all the way to Barrie.

The drive out of Winnipeg was flat. This was the edge of the prairies, where hills and valleys were rare. Caleb found himself looking for a hill, elevation, something as a landmark, but the road ran straight to the horizon. There weren't many trees, and the sky was wide over his head. He had his sunglasses on, since they were driving east and the rising sun came straight through the windshield.

Alana soon dropped off to sleep. He was pleased for her sake, but the drive was boring here. No turns, and cruise control took care of the acceleration. While he had some books he could listen to, he didn't want to disturb the woman sleeping beside him.

Expecting there wouldn't be much radio coverage, he'd downloaded a variety of audiobooks onto his phone that he could play through the vehicle's Bluetooth system. Would she like any of the books he'd chosen? Would their tastes in reading or music coincide? He hoped they would. Just for the convenience of this trip. Right.

After the first hour, the terrain started to change. They were approaching the Canadian Shield, an area of forests and rocks, with cold lakes and few people. By the time they crossed the border into Ontario, they were surrounded by trees.

Caleb distracted himself by watching the traffic behind him. Driving the long straightaways wasn't entertaining, but it meant that if anyone were following them, he'd have a good chance of visualization. He'd checked the SUV for tracking devices.

With only one route they could take, the man who wanted Alana could have gone ahead and be waiting for them anywhere. This trip would be safer, easier, if they weren't doing this undercover. If he could reveal himself and get help from the OPP, who patrolled these roads. He didn't like not being able to trust his fellow officers.

Alana woke up not long after they entered Ontario. She stretched and looked around. "Wow. There are so many trees. And hills."

Caleb laughed. "This is closer to what I think of as normal. Your part of the country is flat."

"Did you know that there are places in Saskatchewan where, when you're driving at night, if you see headlights, you can't tell if they're on the same road as you are or not?"

"That is…not anything I've ever come across. Not sure I like it."

"But the sky is so big. Nothing obstructs it."

"You like that."

Alana nodded.

"But don't you miss trees?"

"We have trees."

"Not like this." He indicated their surroundings.

They passed the time through Kenora and on the first bit of highway east of there comparing the different geographies they were familiar with. Alana had never gone skiing anywhere with real slopes, but Caleb gave the prairies full points for being an easy place to learn to drive a stick shift.

They stopped at a truck stop to let Rex out for a run, and to eat their lunch at the outdoor eating area. Alana avidly examined their surroundings. "Mom and I never traveled far. I thought she was just a homebody. I guess I know why now."

Caleb had been scanning the other vehicles that came into the parking lot, making a mental inventory to check against the next time they stopped. "You'll be able to travel now, if you want. Once you get your ID replaced."

Alana shrugged. "I guess. I haven't thought about the future, not beyond this trip. There's so much in the past to deal with first."

Caleb noted the sorrow on Alana's face. "Do you think your mother ever planned to tell you?"

Alana swallowed the last of her drink and set it on the picnic table. "I don't know when, if she was. I understand why she didn't, when I was a kid. Kids sometimes blurt things out, and to protect me, I needed to be kept in the dark. But when I went to university, or when I came back and started working—those would have been good times to tell me.

"Then, she had her stroke. The first one affected her memory and her ability to speak. Maybe she wanted to tell me then but couldn't. She often was frustrated that she couldn't communicate. Maybe she always planned to keep it a secret."

"Maybe she was embarrassed."

Alana cocked her head. "Embarrassed?"

"Your father was a criminal. She may not have wanted you to know that, or to learn he wasn't the imaginary person you admired. Since she testified, she knew what he was doing, and didn't stop it."

Alana reached down and stroked Rex's head. The dog sat beside her, leaning against her legs.

"Maybe. I'll never know, will I?"

Caleb met her gaze. "How much does that matter?"

Alana shrugged. "I don't know. I'm still trying to understand it. I'm angry and hurt, and kind of sorry for her, and I'm looking at everyone around me, wondering who knew and didn't tell me. What they think of me. Which is stupid, but it's making me suspicious. I trusted everything Mom told me, and the life I had, and it wasn't true.

"If you believe nature over nurture, does that mean I might break the law? Take shortcuts for money? Have I done that and justified it somehow?"

Caleb leaned over and gripped her hands, which had been twisting her water bottle in circles.

"Alana."

He waited until she looked at him.

"I repeat this, because you need to know. You're the same person now as you were a week ago, or a month ago, or a year ago. If you'd been going to lead a life of crime, you would have already started. You're a good person. I know that because of how you've dealt with me, and Rex." And the research that had been done on her, but he couldn't say that. He didn't want to anyway. He wanted this to be the two of them. "If I told you my father had been a criminal, would you back away from me?"

Her mouth opened, but she didn't speak.

"He wasn't, in case you wondered, but I'd still be my own person, still responsible for my own decisions and choices, if he had been. Just like you've made choices and decisions, and none of them have crossed any lines, as far as I can tell."

She squeezed his hands. "Thank you. I needed to hear that. I'm grateful that you're one person I can count on, who I know had no idea who my father was or what had happened with my mother and me. I trust you to be objective."

Caleb had never felt worse about himself. Alana deserved to hear the truth, to have some honesty from him, but before he could break his cover, Rex stood up, growling.

Caleb checked what the dog was looking at. Or smelling or hearing. Something had triggered his protective impulses, and Caleb wasn't going to ignore that. Unfortunately, he didn't have heightened smell or hearing, and he couldn't see anything to give him pause.

It reminded him that Alana needed protection now, more than anything else. If he did tell her the truth, she might not trust him. Until they got somewhere safe, where he knew there were people around her who weren't implicated in a cover-up or her father's crime, he needed her to trust him so that he could protect her.

Chapter Twelve

"I agree, *All Creatures Great and Small* is a charming book, but I don't want to listen to anything work-related when I'm kind of on holiday." Alana was pretending she was taking a trip for fun, not on a quest to find a hidden thing that had put her in danger. "What about something by Mick Herron? They made his books into that spy series."

"No, I don't want anything— I mean, that might remind us of what we're doing."

Alana frowned. She hadn't connected a spy story with her own situation.

Caleb scrolled down to another offering. "How about this one? *The Best Laid Plans* by Terry Fallis. It won the Stephen Leacock award for humor. My dad loves this."

Alana nodded, since something to lighten things up would be good. She'd been relieved when Caleb suggested they listen to a book, since the drive was getting boring. At first, the contrast to the scenery she'd grown up with had kept her watching as the kilometers flew by. They passed through long stretches of tall trees lining the highway, hiding almost everything else. They'd driven through a section where there'd been a fire. Although time had obviously passed, the charcoal stubs of the trees and the desolation of the landscape had been moving. Sad, but the new growth coming back reminded her of the power of nature, an indication of the power of God. Man could make so much, but a forest fire was something men couldn't always control, try as they might. And man wasn't the one bringing the landscape back to life.

But after a while, with nothing to watch but trees, things became monotonous. Caleb had talked before their lunch break, but he was quiet after, and she didn't want to break his concentration if he needed to keep his eyes on the road and his mind on what they were doing. It didn't escape her notice that he checked the rearview mirror often. There wasn't a lot of traffic, but he kept tabs on what there was.

They drove through Thunder Bay midafternoon. It was a larger town on Lake Superior, but they weren't there to be tourists, and Caleb kept moving. The drive was more remote than she'd expected. There were long distances of flat stretches on the prairies, but the fields were mostly all in use. The distance between houses was long, but there were signs of civilization everywhere.

Here, it was nature without any indications of human settlement. It was beautiful, but also, when someone was possibly following them, a little daunting. If something happened to their vehicle, it could be a long wait for assistance. There were no homes nearby to ask for help.

They stopped at a take-out stand in a small town

called Marathon on Lake Superior. Alana was happy to get out of the car and stretch her legs. Rex jumped out of the SUV as soon as Caleb released him, just as pleased to move.

"You okay?" Alana asked Caleb as he moved his shoulders back, working the tension out of them.

"Yeah. Some coffee to go once we've eaten, and I think we can get as far as Wawa tonight."

Alana refused to let the sigh escape. Despite her curiosity about Wawa, the town known for the giant Canada Goose statue, she was ready to be done with driving for the day. She couldn't complain. Caleb was doing this for her. Taking time off his research, putting wear and tear on his vehicle, spending money. If he wanted to push on to Wawa, then they'd push on to Wawa.

They grabbed food and water for Rex, and Alana sat at a picnic table with the dog while Caleb went to get them burgers from the stand. He kept an eye on any vehicles pulling in, but there were only two. One was a young family, one an older couple. Alana didn't think her would-be abductors fit either of those descriptions.

Caleb came back with burgers and fries. Alana didn't care about the quality—she was hungry. They gathered up their wrappers once they were done.

"We should give Rex a bit of exercise. If we're driving on to Wawa, it'll be dark once we get there, and you won't want us walking around then."

Caleb considered and nodded. "I think a walk will do me good as well."

Alana was not looking forward to returning to the car just yet.

A former pulp-and-paper town, the place wasn't large. The views of the lake, the same they'd caught sight of in Thunder Bay, were breathtaking. They left the car at the stand and walked down toward the water. Alana watched Rex, not wanting to push the dog too far while he was still recuperating. Rex, except for the bandage, gave no indication that there was anything wrong with him.

Alana relaxed. She was fond of the dog, already, and could see that Caleb was warming up to him as well. The way he reached down to touch the dog's head, or steer him around any possible hazards.

"You should talk to someone about Rex."

Caleb frowned down at the dog. "Talk to someone?"

"I mentioned it before. He's been trained, and you should check out what he's been trained for. Your uncle—"

"Great-uncle."

"Should have left some instructions. Dogs can be dangerous, and you need to know how to make him stand down."

Caleb looked away from her and Rex. "Yeah, I should. Once we're settled, I'll take care of it."

His shoulders had tensed up again, and Alana wondered why. Was there some kind of family drama about this? Someone else who'd wanted to claim Rex? If so, why had Caleb insisted on taking him when he'd never had a dog before? She couldn't ask him. Not now. Maybe when all this was over. When they were back in Winnipeg, and he would be able to do what he'd come there for. Start on his research and...

Would he still want to spend time with her? They'd been forced into closeness by the attacks. Did Caleb mind? Was she taking advantage of him?

She hoped not. She liked Caleb. A lot. She'd like to

keep spending time with him. She was attracted to him and trusted him. Maybe some of that was because of the circumstances, but maybe not. Once they dealt with this situation her parents had left behind, maybe they could spend time together just for the sake of being together. See if this attraction would lead anywhere. Assuming he felt attracted to her. She wasn't in the best place to figure that out right now.

"We should head back." Caleb pulled to a halt and turned to retrace their steps to the vehicle. Caleb had Rex's lead, and with the narrow sidewalks, the three of them couldn't walk side by side. Alana let the two of them go ahead, and while her thoughts wandered, she watched them.

Caleb was scanning their surroundings, often looking back, checking for any signs of danger. Alana looked around as well but couldn't see anything. Would she even spot something if it was there? That wasn't her expertise, but it did seem to be Caleb's. Was that something he'd done in the army?

Rex was just as alert. She noted his gait, the position of his tail, his coat—all things that could indicate health problems, but Rex was recovering well from his injury. He was watching the surroundings just like Caleb. God had provided her with two able protectors.

They returned to the take-out shack where they'd eaten. Caleb stopped beside the SUV and looked at the couple of vehicles in the parking lot but didn't seem to see anything. Rex however, stiffened, one paw lifted, and stared at their vehicle. Alana pressed close to them.

He whined and caught Caleb's attention. Caleb backed up, taking the dog and Alana with him.

"What's going on?" Alana asked, careful to keep her voice low.

"Something's upset Rex."

"That much I could see for myself. What do you think it is?"

They were now a hundred feet away from the SUV.

"I don't know, but I think he's scented something. Maybe drugs, or a bomb or a cadaver."

Alana whirled to face Caleb. "A bomb? Wouldn't someone tell you if your great-uncle had adopted a bomb-sniffing dog?"

Caleb didn't meet her gaze, eyes still traveling around the area. "Rex is retired. I just don't know what he's retired from."

"Was your great-uncle a cop? Was that why he adopted Rex?"

Caleb shrugged. "Those dogs retire, right? Anyone could adopt them."

Alana shook her head. "No, not just anyone. I thought Rex might have had some training in guarding, but you're saying he's…maybe sniffing out drugs or a bomb? Would they put a bomb in our vehicle?"

She knew she'd been at risk, but not that her life was in jeopardy. If these people would bomb Caleb's vehicle, then this was way more than she could handle. More than she and Caleb, who was another civilian, could handle. They had to get help.

Caleb stiffened when she'd asked her last question, but then his shoulders had dropped, and he'd turned to face her. "No, you're right. No one would do that. A bomb—that's overkill. Excuse the unintentional pun."

Alana wasn't in a place to appreciate humor.

"These people want information that you have. So

blowing up the car wouldn't be in their best interests. And we don't have drugs, and there are no dead bodies involved as far as I know. I'm overreacting, I'm sure."

Better overreacting than underreacting. "What do we do? Just drive on to Wawa?"

"I'll ask at the burger stand, see if anyone was messing with the vehicle. We can check what Rex wants to do. Then yeah, I'd like to get moving again."

She hadn't been looking forward to more driving, but now she wanted to be on their way as soon as possible.

They returned to the lot and approached the vehicle with caution. Rex growled, low in his chest, and circled the SUV, then sat. Whatever had upset him, he didn't see a threat now.

Caleb passed the leash to Alana and went back to the stand. Alana rested a hand on the dog's head. "You sure we're okay now? You gave us a bit of a scare there. I wish we knew just what you were capable of."

Rex leaned against her.

Caleb returned. "No one noticed anything, but they weren't paying attention. Cars come and go. Sometimes they order food or drinks, sometimes they just take a break."

Caleb circled the car, doing a check. Alana watched. When he squatted beside the passenger-side rear tire, she tensed.

"Do you see something?"

Caleb shook his head. "This tire's just a little soft. We'll stop and fill it up before we get out on the highway again."

Alana was reluctant to get into the car, but they couldn't stay here. Caleb opened the hatch for Rex, and when the dog went into his crate without hesitation, Alana forced herself to relax. Whatever had spooked Rex was over.

Caleb drove back a couple of blocks to a gas station with an air pump. Alana stayed in the car as he went through the process of filling up the tire. The air pressure pump beeped as it worked, a familiar sound. It paused, and Alana assumed the tire was properly inflated, but Caleb didn't put the hose back, not immediately.

He finally returned it. Then he got back in the SUV but didn't turn the vehicle on. He faced Alana.

"What is it?"

"The tire was a little soft, but not dangerously so. I filled it back up, and when I was screwing the cap back on, I heard air hissing."

"It does that sometimes."

"I know. But the cap *was* on. That wasn't where I heard the air leaking."

Alana waited.

"I listened some more, and it was coming from the back of the tire. I felt around and found a leak on the inside."

"And?"

"It was a smooth slice. Like someone had stuck a knife into the tire, on the inside where we wouldn't see it. Nothing big, not a huge leak, but the tire would be running flat before we got to Wawa."

They'd have to pull off to change the tire. And the sides of these roads were narrow and desolate.

"Do we have a spare? Is it damaged, too?"

"We have one, and I'll check on it. But even if the spare and the other tires are all fine, we'd have to stop and change it. And we'd be on the side of the road, odds are in a lonely spot, which would be great if someone wanted to get to us."

Alana's heart beat wildly. "You think someone did this on purpose? Trying to get to me?"

Caleb nodded. "Maybe I'm wrong, and it's just damage from a rock or something, but I don't want to take a chance. I want to check all the tires and replace this one."

"I agree."

"But that's not going to happen at this time of day in a small town, so we'll need to find a place to stay for the night here."

Oh. Of course.

Alana reached into her purse. "I can look and see what's available for overnight accommodations. Ones that will take a dog." She stopped. "I don't have a lot of data, though."

She'd gotten Mauve to pick her up a new pay-as-you-go phone, a cheapie, instead of replacing her stolen phone with the same phone number, as a precaution. She wasn't sure how traceable a phone number could be if someone knew what they were doing. Once she was back in Winnipeg, she could get her old number again.

Caleb paused. He slowly pulled his phone out of his pocket. "You could use mine."

He was reluctant. Was there something on his phone he didn't want her to see? Why not do it himself, unless he thought she might then suspect something?

"You don't have to. We can wait while you do it yourself."

He shook his head. "Sorry, little distracted." He let

the phone recognize his face, and then swiped to a browser and passed it to her.

Alana told herself she was getting paranoid. Maybe his data was expensive. He was paying for this whole trip.

"We'll hope there are some dog-friendly options around. Preferably some that take cash, or PayPal. If you can look for that, I'll talk to the attendant here and see where we can get these tires looked at."

Alana drew in a shuddery breath.

"You okay?" Caleb asked.

"I will be. This is all just so much more than I've ever dealt with before. Is freaking out an appropriate response?"

"It's probably appropriate, but I hope you don't panic. We're doing okay. And it's not just us, right?"

It took Alana a moment to understand what he meant. They had God to call on. "Right. I'll take a moment for a quick prayer and then I'll find us somewhere to spend the night."

"One room, okay?"

Alana stiffened. What was Caleb thinking? Her surprise must have been apparent.

"We need to stick together. It's safer."

Alana nodded. He was correct. She was going to sleep a lot better if she knew Caleb and Rex were close by. Close enough to intercept if anyone tried to get her again.

She prayed.

Chapter Thirteen

The area's hotels and motels weren't big on pets, but Alana managed to find them an Airbnb that would take Rex and accept PayPal, rather than a credit card. Caleb wanted to leave as small a trail as possible. He arranged for the local garage to keep the SUV overnight before doing the tire change in the morning. They caught a cab to the place they were staying, a converted garage at the back of someone's property.

Garage apartments seemed to be a thing on this job. Alana opened the door with the code that had been texted to her, and they went inside. It was clean, though small. Sitting area with kitchenette to the side, one door opening to a bedroom, and the other to a small bath. Everything done in neutral gray tones. Caleb put his bag on the couch.

"Do you want to settle in the bedroom while I clean up?"

Alana eyed his bag before nodding. When he came out of the bathroom after a shower, he found his bag moved to the bed.

Alana held up a hand. "Don't even try. You're bigger

than I am, and you drove all day. *And* you'll be driving all day tomorrow. You need a good rest."

The chivalrous thing would be to insist Alana had the bed. But Caleb was tired, and he needed to be sharp tomorrow. Unless the tire was a freak accident, someone had sabotaged the car. They were being followed closely, and whoever was after them wanted to isolate Alana and Caleb, not just follow them. They wanted to get Alana. He couldn't allow that, so he had to be sharp.

Reluctantly, Caleb agreed to the bed. While Alana took her turn in the shower, he texted Yoxall to let him know what had happened. Yoxall advised caution and promised to have people watching out for them tomorrow.

Alana came out and gave him a severe look.

"Just checking some emails, I promise. Are you ready to call it a day?"

Alana took a pillow from the bed, and a blanket. She dropped them on the couch. "I'm exhausted. It's hard to believe that sitting in a car has wiped me out."

"It's not just the car. There's been a lot of tension."

"For you, too. But could we pray again? It will help me sleep."

It would help him as well.

The next morning brought good news. The garage had the right tire in stock and could replace it quickly. When the softened tire came off, it was obvious that it had been deliberately cut. Caleb checked the SUV out as carefully as he could without attracting notice. The guys in the shop were sure it was just some teenagers getting into trouble. Caleb didn't want to attract attention, but he couldn't make that assumption.

They grabbed food from a coffee shop drive-through and were on their way not too much later than Caleb had hoped. There wasn't much traffic, and he didn't spot anyone conspicuously following them.

All they needed was one good day of traveling—that would get them to Barrie. Barrie was less than two hours from Toronto. There, Caleb had trusted people he could call on. He was too isolated out here. Contacting the OPP might have been worth the risk.

The morning was uneventful. After picking up food at a drive-through in Wawa, they stopped to let Rex do his business and take a short walk. They were back on the road soon after, more of the same two-lane highway with scarcely a car in sight, trees edging up to the roadway. Trees, brush, an occasional car passing, but no signs of habitation.

That was when the temperature warning light came on.

Caleb's hands fisted on the steering wheel. "We've got a problem."

Alana, who'd been staring into the trees, tensed and twisted to look behind them. "What kind of problem?"

"The temp light just came on. It could be a glitch, but this is the summer—it's warm. We can't risk driving with it too long. I have the map downloaded on my phone. Can you check when we next come across a town or garage?"

There was no cell coverage here. Alana picked up his phone, and Caleb turned his face toward her for a moment so she could open it. She clicked on the map app and studied it. "The best I can tell about where we are, we have at least a hundred kilometers before we can get help."

Caleb's adrenaline spiked. "I'm not sure how long it's safe to drive. We should pull over and give the car a chance to cool down. It might just be a maintenance thing, but..."

"But?"

"But it might be sabotage. Something more subtle than the tire. Something I missed. If that's the case, and we're out of coolant, we're in trouble."

Alana drew in a breath. "Okay, what would you normally do in this situation?"

Caleb checked the rearview mirror. "Pull over, check the radiator, call for help."

"Have you seen any other cars lately?"

Caleb shook his head. "No, and there's no one I can see at the moment."

Alana looked at the road passing by them. "Would it be best to do it now?"

Caleb signaled, although there was no traffic to warn about his intentions. He pulled over, coming to a gentle stop. With reluctance, he turned off the car. He reached to the glove box and pulled his gun out. Alana watched with wide eyes as he checked that it was loaded.

"Slide into the driver's seat. If something happens, someone suspicious stops and disables me, you put the vehicle in Drive and go as far as you can before the engine seizes up."

Alana shook her head. "I'm not going to abandon you."

Caleb set the gun on his lap for a moment and took her hand. "If we get to that point, and it's either me or all of us being caught, I'll have a better chance of surviving if you get out of here and call for help. I'm going to give you my phone, and the pin to open it."

If someone had done this on purpose and was now going to attack them, the phone would be of no use to him. "If worst comes to worst, you call the contact Yoxall when you get to a place where they have coverage. This is a guy I trust, and he'll figure out what to do. Tell him everything, okay?"

He recited the code to unlock the phone. Her hands were trembling, and he wanted to tell her it would be okay, that everything would work out. Except that things didn't always work out. He'd never understood why bad things had to happen, and he'd had to leave it to God, doing his part to make things better. It was harder to trust God with Alana. She'd become more than a job, more than a mission. And she was going to hate him when she found out he'd been using her.

Still, the most important thing was that she was safe to hate him.

He picked up his gun again and opened his door. He listened for the sounds of another vehicle. When he heard nothing but the wind rustling in the trees and crickets in the background, he slid out and stood, waiting for her to cross into his seat. She hesitated, but he refused to move. When she did as he'd asked, he closed the door. He checked again, looking for traffic in either direction. Then he slipped forward to check the engine of the SUV.

As soon as he lifted the hood he knew they had a coolant problem. Steam wafted off the radiator. He couldn't investigate the problem until the car cooled off. They were stuck here for a while. Stuck, with no cell coverage, all alone.

The vehicle was a rental, and fairly new. It shouldn't have any issues with the cooling system. Someone could have loosened the valve to let the coolant out until the level got too low to cool the engine. He should have checked the car better this morning. There were just so many things that could go wrong...

He heard tires, and a car slowed as it passed them. Despite the warmth of the day, goose bumps rose on his skin. He couldn't see much of the people inside. Two men, sunglasses and ball caps pulled low. Could just be their normal wear, or they could be trying to disguise how they looked. Caleb turned to face them, sliding the gun he'd tucked into the back of his shorts into his hand. He risked a glance at Alana. She had her hands on the steering wheel, and her gaze on the car as it pulled to a stop ahead of them.

There was no movement from the car. Caleb considered options. He could tell Alana to drive off, but she wasn't a cop he could give commands to, and she'd argue about it. Another option was Rex. The dog had proven he was well trained, but he was no match for a gun and a man willing to use it.

Maybe he should just get back in the car and drive off. See how far they got with the overheated engine. It wouldn't be any great distance. If this wasn't the people after Alana, they needed help with the disabled vehicle before those people did show up.

Caleb kept the gun out of sight beside him and waited for the men in the car to make their move.

The passenger door opened, and the man inside stood, turning toward them. He was big, and Caleb thought he saw the glint of metal from a gun in the hand he was holding to his side. His stomach tightened. He kept his arm behind him, slid the safety off his weapon and took a step forward. His first priority was Alana. If there was shooting, would she duck? He tried to watch her with his peripheral vision while he kept his eyes on the car in front of them.

Her eyes were open, but he saw her mouth moving. She was…praying?

The driver's door opened. Another man got out, and this time, there was no mistaking the gun. The two men exchanged a glance, then took a step toward them.

His heart was pounding, adrenaline rushing into his muscles. He took a long breath, about to signal Alana to duck, when the two men paused. Their heads tilted. Caleb heard another car, approaching from behind them. He flattened against the driver's door, trying to watch the men ahead while seeing who was coming from behind. If the men in front had allies, Caleb and Alana were in serious trouble.

Which vehicle would be more of a threat, and how would he know?

Chapter Fourteen

Hᴇ stood as if frozen as the car appeared around the trees of the corner behind. It braked sharply and came to a halt behind them, gravel spraying from the rapid stop. When Caleb glanced forward, there was no longer any sign of weapons in the hands of the men ahead.

Not allies coming in from behind to trap them?

He narrowed his eyes to get a better look at the car behind. A late-model sedan, nothing fancy. The doors opened, and a white-haired man with a beer belly got out from the driver's side. A woman of the same age exited from the passenger door, and the two rushed forward. Caleb's grip tightened on his gun.

The man spoke first, stopping a safe distance back. He was smiling, arms relaxed at his sides. "Is everything okay? Are you folks in trouble? This is a pretty isolated stretch of highway."

The garrulous older couple weren't the threat he was afraid of. There was no sign of a weapon, and their hands were visible. The woman chastised the man. Husband? "Randall Hoffler, don't be silly. No one stops here for more than a minute if they're not in trouble."

Hoffler. That was one of the names Yoxall had given him. They weren't a threat. But the men ahead—if they were after Alana, would they try to take her with even the Hofflers here? Caleb maintained his stance leaning against the SUV where he could watch the men with guns while responding to the Hofflers.

"I've got some car trouble. I think the men in the car ahead were stopping to help."

The man on the passenger side was still watching them, the driver having returned to the vehicle.

"That's most kind of them. In a remote place like this, people have to look out for each other. But you probably don't need both of us, so we can assist you, if they have places to be. Unless they're mechanics? My husband can't fix your car, but we can give you a lift if you need it."

"That's a lovely offer. I think we should take you up on it."

Even though Caleb and the Hofflers were speaking to each other, Hoffler had his eyes pinned on the car ahead of him, the same as Caleb. Maybe it was nothing, but he suspected Hoffler had been a cop. He even more strongly suspected that the men ahead had put the SUV out of commission by tampering with the cooling system.

"Why don't you come with us, and we can send a tow truck once we reach the next town. Just bring all your valuables along." That was Mr. Hoffler speaking again.

"We have a dog."

"Oh, we love dogs. That's not a problem. What kind of dog do you have? What's its name?" The woman he assumed was Mrs. Hoffler had a voice that carried.

The man standing beside the car ahead slid inside

and closed the door. The car pulled out and took off down the road heading southeast.

"Well, they weren't talkative." Mrs. Hoffler sounded offended.

"No, they weren't, were they?" Caleb knocked on the window of the driver's door and pointed down. Alana, her glance moving between the car leaving ahead of them and the couple who'd come up from behind, rolled the window down.

"Caleb?"

"This nice couple have offered us a ride."

She looked worried. He smiled at her, hoping she realized that he only suggested this because it was a safe move. He couldn't tell her why he trusted this couple without revealing his ties to Yoxall, and he didn't know how much Yoxall had shared with the Hofflers. They might only have been told to watch out for them, not why. It was safer not to say anything in front of the pair.

Alana gave him wide eyes, and he knew she was asking if it was safe. He gave a short nod, hoping she'd accept that he was confident, and stepped back.

Alana gave the Hofflers a smile. "Thanks for rescuing us. Do you know where the nearest place is to get a tow?"

"It's about a hundred klicks. This is not a good place for a breakdown, that's for sure. How far are you two heading?"

Caleb moved to the back of the vehicle and opened the hatch. Rex was sitting up in his crate, ears perked. Caleb opened the gate and snapped on his leash. Rex hopped down, gaze on the Hofflers.

"Isn't he a handsome boy?" Mrs. Hoffler said. Rex

looked from her to her husband, but his hackles stayed lowered, and he didn't pull on his lead.

"He's new to me, but we're learning to get along."

"What happened to him?" Mrs. Hoffler spotted the bandages. Her husband was assisting Alana in taking their bags from the back seat.

"An accident. He's recovering well."

Mrs. Hoffler frowned. "Are you sure he's okay?"

Caleb smiled at her. "Alana is a vet, so she's been taking good care of him."

"Oh, your wife is a vet—how nice."

Alana's voice cut through. "Oh, no—we're not married." A pause. "Or together. I mean, we're traveling together but we're not dating. We've only known each other a short time. Like, a week."

Mrs. Hoffler's expression softened. "I didn't mean to make you uncomfortable. I apologize. But it doesn't always take a long time. We knew right away. Forty years married now."

Caleb's cheeks warmed, and Alana's had a pink tinge to them that he didn't think was the result of the sun. There'd been something growing between them—an attraction, but also a connection.

Working undercover was how he would carry on his family's legacy. This was not the time to start a romantic relationship. If Alana would even consider it once she knew the truth.

"We're embarrassing them, hon. Let's get their stuff in the car and get them some help."

The car was comfortable and full-sized, but there wasn't room for Rex's crate. Once they'd put their bags in the trunk, Alana, Caleb and Rex all cozied up in the back seat, Rex playing duenna in the middle.

Mrs. Hoffler carried the conversation as they drove on. She didn't ask questions about them or what they were doing on this highway, which confirmed to Caleb that the Hofflers knew he was undercover, and they weren't making his job harder. Instead, she rattled on about her family, and the area, and people they knew. Caleb, sitting behind Mrs. Hoffler, saw her husband give her an amused look, and guessed that she didn't normally talk this much.

When they arrived in the next town, the garage was closed for the day.

Mrs. Hoffler sighed. "That man has no business closing up early. He just wants to get out fishing."

"There's not a lot of work here?"

She shook her head. "Not a lot of people, so not a lot of work."

They pulled the car to a stop outside the garage. Alana took Rex for a stroll around the front of the building. Her mouth was set in a straight line, and she looked around as if searching for answers from their surroundings.

Caleb would have liked to talk privately to the Hofflers, but he didn't want to step any further away from Alana. They might have advice or information for him, but that wasn't something she should hear.

"Well." Mr. Hoffler spoke for the first time in a while. "We can take you on to the Sault."

Caleb knew he meant Sault Sainte Marie, the next major city.

"You could definitely get some help there. Or, if you're in a rush, we can take you as far as Sudbury. Either place, you could get a rental if you needed. And a place to stay the night."

Caleb had half expected an offer of a bed from the couple. But he didn't know where they lived, and convincing Alana it was safe to stay with them without breaking his cover might be tricky.

"Alana?" Caleb called, and she and Rex returned. "The Hofflers have offered to take us to Sault Sainte Marie or Sudbury, where they're going. We can find a place to stay, get a rental car, and I can arrange for someone to take care of the SUV."

Alana gave the Hofflers a grateful smile. "That is incredibly generous of you."

Mrs. Hoffler smiled. "You just pay it forward someday. I like to put good karma out there into the world."

Caleb knew it was more than that. They had safe passage a little further on their trip, and that was enough for now.

It had been another long, stressful day and Alana was tired. She was grateful to the Hofflers for bringing them to Sudbury. She'd been afraid the couple would offer to drive them to a hotel. The idea made her edgy. Caleb was trusting them, but she didn't understand why, when he'd been so cautious before. When she'd found a private moment to ask him, he'd said they didn't fit the profile of the previous people who'd abducted her.

They were trusting a lot in that small detail. She'd relaxed once the couple had left them at a park, with Rex and their bags, rather than taking them to a hotel.

Alana did more work on Caleb's phone, saving the limited data on her prepaid burner phone, and found another Airbnb they could stay in with Rex. After confirming with Caleb, she booked the place, and they arranged for transportation. Their driver's eyes grew big when he saw Rex, but he didn't say anything—maybe worried they'd sic Rex on him if he complained.

This time they were in a basement apartment below some shops. People were passing on the street, and Rex sat at attention, ears up, until they settled for the night. Alana won the argument about the bed again. Rex curled up beside the sofa once she'd settled in, and after a prayer offering gratitude and asking for more assistance, Alana fell asleep.

She was the first to wake in the morning. When she sat up, Rex did the same. She smiled at the dog and smoothed his fur. If his wound still looked good, they could do without the bandages now. She removed them gently, and Rex appeared relieved to have them gone.

"You've been a good boy with those," Alana whispered. Rex stood and crossed to the door. He whined, came back to nudge her and returned to the door. Alana glanced over at the bedroom, but Caleb must still be asleep. He probably needed all he could get. Today they should arrive in Barrie, and maybe, by the end of the day, she'd have figured out the place her mother had been talking about. Where her parents had their first and last date. This could all be over.

She'd fallen asleep in what she'd been wearing, shorts and a T-shirt. They hadn't showered last night. Since they were close to Barrie now, with only about three hours left to drive, they'd agreed to take it easy this morning: shower, have breakfast, then find a car and be on the road again.

They were past the isolated part of the drive. From here on out, there would be towns and cities with lots of people around. That should make it easier for them to lose whoever was following them.

They, whoever they were, would have been able to identify Caleb's car from Winnipeg, but now she and Caleb would have a rental and could, she hoped, lose their followers. And even if that didn't work, there would be people around them most of the time, making an attack less likely. The two men who'd stopped hadn't done anything with the Hofflers there, and from now on they had plenty of Hofflers in the area.

Maybe the worst was over?

Yesterday, when the SUV had overheated and Caleb had taken out his gun, had been one of the most terrifying moments of her life. That, the attempted abduction and robbery, and when she knew she was losing her mother. What if they'd escaped the men now, and wouldn't see them again? Alana's spirits lifted at the thought. They'd just try to track down the hidden whatever, and then…

Then they could return to Winnipeg. Caleb could settle into the garage apartment and do his research while Alana got back to the clinic. Maybe they would be able to spend time together, normal time. Dates. Going to church. She was smiling as she slid on her sandals and crossed to the door where Rex was waiting.

She opened it quietly, and, with Rex on the lead, went up the steps to the small parking pad. She scanned the area and watched Rex for signs of concern. Since he was relaxed, she took him to a corner to relieve himself.

He'd been holding it in. She hoped no one would be upset at the mess, but there were strays in every city, and this was undoubtedly not the first or last time a dog would mark the area.

Suddenly the door to the rental slammed open, and Alana heard someone rushing up the steps. She turned to run, and Rex leaped in front of her.

"Alana!" It was Caleb, sounding breathless. He had his gun in his hand.

Her breathing stopped for a moment, and fear almost paralyzed her. "What's wrong?" Who was after her and what did Caleb plan for them to do? His feet were bare, and his shirt misbuttoned. He stared at her, eyes wide.

"Are you okay?"

Alana pitched her voice low, in case someone was listening. "We're fine. Rex had to pee. What's happened?"

Caleb leaned over, resting his hands, including the one holding the pistol, on his thighs. "I woke up, and you were gone."

The air rushed out of her lungs. This was on her. "I'm sorry, Caleb. I wanted you to get as much sleep as you could, and Rex needed to go out."

He drew in a long breath and straightened. "Never leave without telling me."

Alana had been careful. She'd checked her surroundings, and so had Rex. But Caleb was helping her out of the goodness of his heart. He was putting himself in danger, and his dog had been injured protecting her. The least she could do was not scare him.

"I'm sorry. I won't do it again."

Rex nudged her. "Should we go back in? Do you want to sleep any more?"

Caleb stood back, letting her go first. "I'm pretty awake now. Why don't we get ready and find a car rental place?"

Was he angry with her? Did he regret helping her? He'd gone over and above what anyone could ask of a new acquaintance. Was he just that helpful a guy or was he…

Alana shook her head. No, he couldn't be using her. She didn't know him, and maybe she'd been too quick to trust him, but Mr. Conners had vouched for him. She'd prayed. She couldn't second-guess things now.

The morning didn't seem as bright. Alana sighed as she urged Rex back indoors.

Chapter Fifteen

Getting a replacement vehicle went smoothly. Caleb chose another SUV, and Alana had to let him pay. Did he have enough money? She had no way to access her own yet. By the time they were back in Winnipeg, she should have a bank card and be able to withdraw from her accounts. Regaining that independence would feel good. She'd pay him back every cent, and would offer him more if she thought there was any possibility he'd accept it.

The ride to Barrie passed mostly in silence. She suspected Caleb was still upset about her vanishing act this morning. She understood. If she'd woken up and found Rex and him missing…she'd have been terrified. Giving him time to settle down felt like the best option. Meanwhile, she was trying to pin down the stories her mother had told her.

She closed her eyes, picturing her mother's beloved face. How could she have held on to this secret for so many years?

Alana had had questions about her father, especially once she'd been at school and other kids had their dads around. Her mother told her that her father had loved her, but he'd been in a car accident and gone to heaven. For most of the time, though, the man had been in prison. Her mother not only knew about it but had testified against him. Did that mean she hadn't loved him anymore?

Looking back with the eyes of an adult, she appreciated the times when her mother had told her she didn't want to talk about her father anymore, that it made her sad. She tried to remember back to high school, the time when her father would have really died. Could she remember her mother reacting to that news, still keeping it from her then?

Maybe. There was an unprecedented time when her mother had taken a week off work, sick days. Alana, an oblivious seventeen-year-old, had mostly been concerned that she might get the same bug. It could have been grief, not the flu, that her mother had endured. They could have been a support for each other if her mother had told her. But she hadn't. And Alana couldn't ask her why.

She couldn't remember any stories about her dad after that time. As if by mutual agreement, Alana hadn't asked and her mother hadn't offered. Before high school, when she was young, and her mother must have been struggling, as a single parent with a new identity, her mother had talked. Perhaps she'd needed to keep that connection?

There had been one Christmas...when Alana had been feeling the lack of a father and asked if she couldn't get one for Christmas. That must have been soon after they moved to Winnipeg, when Alana thought a parent was something that could show up with the Christmas tree.

That was when her mother had told her about meeting her father. Her mother had gone to the local drive-in theater with some friends. Her father had been visiting some buddies in Barrie. There had been a large group of teenagers at the drive-in that night, and her mother had met her dad when they lined up for the snack bar and ordered the same thing.

Mountain Dew and Twizzlers. Her mother had always loved those.

Did she remember it correctly after all this time? She was pretty sure they'd also had their last date there. Yes, that was right. Her mother said the first and last date were at the same place. They'd gone back to revisit that first meeting. Then her father had…not died. Instead, he'd been arrested and gone to prison.

But she didn't know if there had been many drive-in movie theaters in the area. Her mom lived in Barrie, so it had to be close to that city. She knew her teenage parents-to-be had thought Mountain Dew and Twizzlers was an unusual combination, but most theaters would have carried the two products, and how would she be able to check a menu from a drive-in movie theater from more than twenty-five years ago?

She'd looked online before they'd left and found five theaters within sixty-five kilometers of the city of Barrie at that time. None of the names rang a bell. It was unlikely that her mother would have told her the name anyway—the emphasis of the story had been the initial meeting and return visit. Alana had listed the theaters and their addresses in a note, and thought they could start at the closest one, because she wasn't sure kids would drive more than forty kilometers for an evening out. How far would her grandparents have allowed her mother to go?

But a drive-in movie theater would cover a lot of ground if they found the right one. She needed details. Bits of the story that would give clues as to the location of not just the theater, but where in that drive-in her mother might have hidden something valuable.

The concession stand was a big part of her mother's story, but that didn't narrow things down since every drive-in would have that. The groups of kids had been able to spend time together. So maybe less of a family place? Would there be a difference in the theaters? What could her mother possibly have told her that might help her identify it?

It was all pointless. Whatever the evidence was, and wherever it might be, she wasn't going to find it. She'd dragged Caleb and Rex out for nothing, and now someone wanted to do her harm, just because she thought she'd been smart enough to figure this out.

She felt Caleb's hand on her arm and opened her eyes.

"You okay? You look like you're thinking about a hundred miles an hour over there, and the thoughts aren't good."

She sighed. "I can't do this."

He took his eyes off the road to check on her. "Are you worried about these guys after you?"

She shook her head. "It's not that. I'm kinda hoping we've lost them. I'm trying to come up with anything that could help us find my mother's hiding spot. There are five drive-in movie theaters in the Barrie area that existed then, and each one will cover a lot of space.

And that's only if I'm right, and that's what Mom meant in that letter. And that she did it and didn't just say she had or didn't change her mind later and move it again. Even if that's all true, maybe someone found it, or it's been destroyed or—"

"Alana, take a breath. It's okay."

She clenched her fists. "No, it's not. I've put myself in danger, and you, and Rex has been injured because I thought I knew something, and I don't."

Caleb no longer looked frustrated with her. Now his expression had veered to worried.

"Can you take a breath?"

She glared at him. "You're not going to tell me to calm down, are you?"

He barked out a laugh. "No, that would be the wrong thing to say. I just want to remind you of a couple of things."

Long breath. In, then out. And again. "Okay, what is it?"

"This is not your fault. You didn't start any of it."

"But—"

"No, remember? Someone broke into your house, and then, the first day I got there, someone tried to abduct you. At that point, you didn't know anything about your father and his history. You didn't know about witness protection or that your mother had kept a big secret from you. This started before you tried to help."

Her shoulders unwound a notch. "Okay, that's right. But—"

"Rex was hurt before you had any idea of what was going on. And even when you did find out, you've only tried to help. I offered to assist you, you didn't make me. I'm still doing this voluntarily. I'm curious, I admit, probably more than I should be, and I want to make sure that these people who are trying to hurt you don't get what they want."

Her body relaxed, the spiral of worry dissipating with his words and his concern.

He shot a glance into the rearview mirror. Rex was sleeping on the back seat since they no longer had his crate with them. "Now, you might have a point when it comes to Rex. I dragged him along without asking him, but he likes you. He'd have voted to come if we'd asked him."

Alana turned in her seat. Rex opened one eye, and then wriggled into the seat and went back to sleep.

Caleb's voice turned teasing. "He's not worrying. You shouldn't, either."

"I know, but—"

"*But* you're the one who's asked to pray before we start each day. And at the end of every day, we've been fine."

The thought hit Alana like a shot. She had forgotten that she and Caleb and Rex weren't on their own. She'd asked for guidance, and this was where it had led her. "You're right. I might not have faith in myself, but I have faith in God. Thank you for reminding me."

"See, I knew it was the right call for me to take this trip with you."

Alana turned to him. "I hope you know how grateful I am. I couldn't have done this on my own. I wouldn't be safe here without you."

Caleb met her eyes and she saw something in his expression. Then he wrenched his gaze forward again to the road.

But that look—it warmed her, through and through.

It gave her hope for what might happen once they returned to Winnipeg.

Caleb cleared his throat. "We're almost there. Do you want to find the directions to the first drive-in?"

Alana picked up his phone from the console where he'd left it to charge. They had coverage again, and knowing she could be in touch with the world was a comfort. "I thought we'd check out the closest one first. Okay?"

"That sounds logical to me."

Alana turned on the voice directions to take them there.

They pulled up in front of the first drive-in on her list. They could see the screens, three of them, tilted inward to discourage people from watching from outside the drive-in itself. A fence surrounded the place, with a drive to the entrance. At this time of day, the place was closed and deserted.

Caleb drove the rental vehicle as close as possible, to the head of the drive, as if they were eager customers for a show that wouldn't start for hours. They opened their doors and stepped out. Caleb opened the rear door and allowed Rex to hop down.

Alana noted everything she could from here. There were the three screens. A two-story concession stand, and a playground for kids. It looked like a family type of place. Not quite what Alana had been thinking.

But a look at the movies playing showed that the offerings included more than family and kid movies. With some of those, the superhero and action movies, she could picture high school and college kids hanging out here, a place where they could mingle and not be limited to the friends who fit in their car. And on a hot summer night, there'd be a breeze. Maybe they'd hang out in the playground.

She'd need to compare it to pictures from years ago, see if it had changed. This might be the place. Then again, it might not. How was she ever going to figure this out?

Rex wandered around, sniffing, and lifting his leg occasionally. "I suppose it's too much to think she told you any details about the theater and you've suddenly remembered, eh?" Caleb asked.

Alana smiled, but it wasn't a good effort. "I don't even know what movies were playing. They wouldn't have been the same, but even knowing one might help."

"She didn't tell you?"

"If she did, I've forgotten."

"Do you know what movies were playing those years?"

"No, but I can find out." She held out her hand, and he passed over his phone. She was burning through his data, since she had so little on her phone. She typed in a search in the browser.

That information was easy to come by. She scrolled through the names of films, some classics, some she'd never heard of, and some...

"Titanic!" She looked up at Caleb, phone tight in her hand.

He grinned at her. "My mom loved that one. Kate Winslet, right? You think that was the movie?"

Alana nodded. "I remember now. She said she didn't like the movie they watched the first time she came and met Dad, so he brought her to one he knew she'd like for the return visit. She loved *Titanic*—they'd watched it already at a regular theater but wanted to see it again."

Alana was staring into the distance, the echo of her mother's voice in her head. She shook her head.

Caleb was watching her closely. "Anything else?"

Alana looked around the drive-in where they were. "This has three screens. Are the other drive-ins smaller? 'Cause if there were three movies playing, Mom could have gone to watch a different one that first time, when she didn't like the one movie."

Caleb turned to look over the site again and shrugged.

"This is just the first one we've looked at, so we should probably look at all of them, see what they're like and if you remember any more details. There's no one around this one right now, but I think they're opening up soon. Let's move on, since we can't really look for a potential hiding place. We'll check out the others, and decide which ones look like the best bet. Make a plan from there."

He smiled at her, but her heart sank. Five drive-in movie theaters? How was she going to find where her mother would have hidden something? And what were the odds it would still be around?

Chapter Sixteen

Caleb didn't want to discourage Alana, but he was second-guessing this.

This drive-in covered a lot of ground. Unless Alana could remember more details, he had no idea where they should look. It would have to be someplace that wouldn't be disturbed by normal activity when the place was in service, or it would already have been found. But that left a lot of parking lot, the play area, the space around the concession stand, behind the screen...

Rex pushed up against her. Alana's hand moved to pet him, but it looked like she was getting more comfort out of it than the dog was. Maybe this wasn't the right place, and when they found the right one, she would remember more. After all, once she saw the movie name more things had popped up in her memories.

He didn't need to discourage her. Instead, he focused on the positive—they were getting closer.

"Okay, the next one is Elmvale. We can check it out, and maybe one more today. We'll find a place to stay after that and check the others tomorrow."

Alana moved to the SUV. She opened the back hatch for Rex, and Caleb had the engine going by the time she sat in the passenger seat. She still looked discouraged.

"You know, if we need to, we could use a fleece."

Alana frowned. "A fleece?"

"Remember the story about Gideon? He wasn't sure what to do, so he set out a fleece. We can lay it out overnight and we can ask that it not get covered in dew when we choose the right theater."

Alana chuckled, and he wanted to preen because he'd cheered her up.

"I've a fleece sweater in my bag. We can set it out at Elmvale if we need to."

Caleb put the SUV in Drive. "Let's go."

They were quiet as they approached the Elmvale Drive-In. It was obvious, from a distance, that this place was no longer in use. The screen was missing panels, leaving large gaps in it. The back now read Dri e In, the *v* long gone. The land around it was flat, with only a few scrubby trees near the base of the screen and around the buildings and drive.

Caleb moved slowly up the driveway and turned the corner into the abandoned parking lot. This had been a much smaller business than the last one. Only one screen, with a smaller concession stand. The ticket booth as they passed it was almost engulfed by bushes.

Caleb rolled to a halt in the middle of the lot, leaving space in case anyone else drove in. At the last theater, they had not been far from buildings and businesses, with lots of people nearby. Here it was isolated, and almost spooky. He turned off the vehicle, and they opened their doors, getting out slowly. Rex's nose twitched, probably smelling rabbits or squirrels.

After a scan of the lot showed no indications of other people having used this place for a long time, Caleb walked over to the concession stand. He peered inside. There were holes in the roof, and inside, animals, people and nature had all done their part to make it a mess. Graffiti, animal droppings and seedlings. The smell was bad. No one would have used this for a hiding place. When the theater was operational, this would have had the densest population of workers and moviegoers.

When he turned back, Alana was looking around the lot, as if trying to imagine it when it was a thriving business, with carloads of eager movie fans coming to watch their favorite films. Caleb knew the projector he'd seen parts of through the missing windows wasn't going to show anything again.

"If this is the one your mother was talking about, the good news is that we can poke around all we want, and no one would know, let alone question us. The bad news is that everything of value has been removed or destroyed."

Alana nodded. "This is kinda creepy, isn't it?"

Caleb agreed. The place reminded him that humans could only impose on nature for so long. There were more powerful forces out there.

"I don't suppose this reminded you of anything your mother told you?"

"No. But I could see teenagers driving out here, hanging out together… And there'd only be one movie at a time."

"Ready to check out one more before we call it a day?"

Alana nodded and got back into the SUV.

The third place was another operating, busy theater with three screens. It was just starting to open up when they got there, employees prepping for the shows that night. By mutual agreement they kept going without stopping to check it out further, heading back to Barrie, where Alana had found another Airbnb for them.

She was tired and discouraged. Once they'd followed the directions and unlocked the rental, he suggested she shower while he went to pick up something to eat.

Her eyes moved up to his. "Is that safe?"

He nodded at Rex. "I'll leave him with you. He'll know if anyone is coming long before we would. We're no longer on the only possible road, so I don't think anyone has followed us. I've been watching."

They were in another basement suite. The layout was similar to the other rentals they'd had. Open living area with kitchenette, doors to bedrooms and bathroom.

"If anyone tries to get in, run up the stairs and pound on the connecting door until the homeowners let you in. But I don't think you'll need that."

Caleb needed to call Yoxall and it would be better to do this on his own from the car, where he couldn't be overheard. Alana might like some privacy herself. They'd been in almost constant company with each other for days. Not that he was complaining.

He left Alana with Rex on guard and climbed into

the SUV. At a school parking lot close by, he pulled in and called Yoxall.

"Caleb! Where are you and how are things going?"

"We're in Barrie. Had a couple of close calls, but your friends the Hofflers were lifesavers."

Yoxall grunted. "I talked to him, asked him to check the SUV. He said there was some sabotage done on the cooling system."

Caleb had received the same message from the garage that towed his vehicle in. Either a freak accident had opened the valve on the radiator, or human fingers had. "That was the second time. First time, it was the tire. Looked like the intention was for us to be disabled away from a town. Which means they still want Alana and are still following us."

"Have you spotted them?"

"Not since the Hofflers chased them off. I'm in a rental vehicle, so I assume they can't track us by the plates or make and model and color now. But there's a lot more traffic here, so I don't know for sure if anyone has been following. Nothing obvious, but still."

There was silence. Caleb thought he heard Yoxall scribble on paper, making notes.

"What are your plans now?"

"We're checking out the drive-ins in the area. There are five that were operating at the time we think Alana's mother moved the evidence, and we've looked at three. Two of them are still in operation, but bigger places with three screens. Alana thinks the place we want might be something smaller. The small one we looked at was long abandoned. If that's the place, the evidence may be gone."

Yoxall grunted again. "It's a long shot. But someone

thinks it's worth pursuing enough to go after Alana, so we'll try to stay a step ahead of them. There's enough cell coverage there that we can track your phone. I'll make sure you've got help if you need it."

Caleb felt tension easing out of his body, muscles relaxing for the first time in days. He wasn't on his own anymore—he had resources he could call on. He was used to being part of a team, not operating solo. Another part of undercover work to adjust to.

"Thanks. I'm gonna pick up some food, and we'll stay in for the night. Tomorrow we can check out the other two drive-ins and decide what we should do next."

Yoxall grunted. "How are you doing? Any problems with your cover?"

Caleb didn't answer immediately. He had problems, but not the way Yoxall was asking.

Alana still believed in his story, and he'd had no indication that anyone else had made him for an undercover cop. But he hated lying to Alana. The guilt was a constant irritation. If he told Yoxall that, he could kiss goodbye any chance he had of going undercover in future, and his chance to fulfill his father's dream.

This had to be something other undercover cops struggled with as well. Maybe it was just because usually the people being lied to were the bad guys, the ones you were trying to stop from hurting people. Caleb was lying to one of the good people, and that was a struggle. He was torn between honesty and protection. If he told Alana, she'd be upset. Hurt and betrayed. And then he couldn't keep her safe. Whom would she trust? Not anyone he'd recommend, and if she trusted the wrong person, she'd be at risk.

"Everything is good. Is there any word on Rex's owner? And have you found any information to help me with him yet? It's obvious he has been trained for police work and I don't know how to direct him."

"Right. Sorry, Sawatzky isn't doing well, so I can't ask him." Yoxall sighed. "The original idea was that you'd be sitting in that apartment watching for strangers, not gallivanting around the country with Fowler on your heels. You may need to use Rex again. I'm not sure how that will go—it normally takes a long time to build a partnership between cop and dog. I'll send you information today—I'll make it a priority. You don't have to let anyone know you know, but the dog is an asset if you get in trouble."

Caleb nodded, even though Yoxall couldn't see him.

"Okay, get going. I'll wait to hear from you again."

"Good night, sir."

Caleb let a long breath escape. For better or worse, this should be over soon. Part of him was relieved to think Alana would be safe, and able to return to her normal life. She could go back to Winnipeg, take care of her animals and…

And Caleb, hopefully, would have a successful undercover op under his belt. Maybe they wouldn't find whatever Alana's mother might have hidden, but if they followed this lead as far as they could, then she would have no information of value to anyone.

He'd never need to see her again. She might never want to, once she knew who he really was. That shouldn't make him feel…devastated. Was that normal for under-cover work? Or was he fonder of her than he should be?

He put the truck in gear and headed to the restaurant to pick up his order. Whether it was just his job or not, he was anxious to get back, make sure she and Rex were safe, and spend as much time with her as he could.

Chapter Seventeen

Alana was combing out her wet hair when Caleb returned. He knocked on the door, and she opened it quickly. Her worried expression turned to a smile when she saw him.

"That smells so good."

Caleb passed her the bag. "You should have checked who was at the door."

Alana was halfway to the small kitchen to grab plates and utensils. "Rex did it for me. He stood at the door, wagging his tail. He only does that for people he knows."

Caleb passed a hand over Rex's head. "He's worth his weight in kibble."

"And then some." Alana was back with the dishes, since the place was tiny. "Which one is mine?"

"Whichever you want. I got a variety—more than we can eat, but we can always warm them up for breakfast."

"Excellent plan. Sorry, Rex, none of this is for you."

Rex turned sad eyes toward Caleb. Caleb raised his hands. "She's the doctor. I'm not going to give you any of that without her say-so."

Rex sighed and dropped his head on his paws.

"I had a thought." Alana spread everything Caleb had ordered on the counter, and cut a burrito and a quesadilla in half, taking one part of each and adding them to one of the plates.

"Hit me."

She glanced up, a teasing smile on her face, and Caleb wanted to freeze that image in his brain. "We should watch *Titanic*."

Caleb froze. His mother might have watched the movie over and over again, but he had avoided it. He preferred action movies, or comedies. Not long-drawn-out romantic disasters.

Her smile vanished. "Or I can watch it on my own. I can find it streaming somewhere, I'm sure."

She shrugged, and he felt like a heel. He reached for a plate and took the halves that Alana had left behind. "You think this might help you figure out where your mother hid whatever she was talking about in that letter?"

"Maybe. I don't think it can hurt. When I saw the movie title, I remembered that was what they saw that last date. Maybe seeing the movie will nudge my brain into more memories. But I won't inflict it on you."

He should help her remember anything she could. If he was honest, he also wanted her to smile at him again. "No, I'll watch with you."

She rolled her eyes. "You don't have to. It obviously isn't the kind of movie you like."

She was right, but the other option, of her wrapped up in the movie with headphones on while he did something on his own, had no appeal. He didn't have much time with her left. They couldn't spend too many nights watching *Titanic* and looking at drive-in movie theaters before there was nothing more to do.

They could narrow the list down to which movie theater it might be, and see if they could figure out where something could be hidden. But unless they got lucky, they'd have to bring in the authorities to get a metal detector, or a trained dog. He doubted that Rex was trained to look for videotapes or jewelry. Had Marie Campbell found something to protect the items from the elements? Or was there nothing left to find?

Caleb nudged Alana's foot with his. "It's probably good for my character. And maybe I can help. See something that leads us to the hiding place."

Alana crossed her arms. "You do realize this movie takes place more than a hundred years ago, right? There are no drive-in movie theaters in it."

"What else am I going to do?"

It didn't bring back that smile, but when Alana sat on the couch and Caleb joined her, he thought he saw her lips quirk. Just a bit, but he'd take anything he could. The rental had a smart TV, and Alana worked her way through the options available until she was able to find a service streaming the movie, an edited version that was suitable for all audiences. They settled on the couch, with their food and drinks, Rex sprawled at their feet. It was a cozy, homey break to what had become their usual routine. Caleb liked it.

He couldn't say the same about the movie. He had little patience with the scenes that showed the obnoxious boyfriend and was more invested in the sets revealing what the ship would have looked like. He wanted to get past the drama and get to the action when the ship hit the iceberg.

Before that, they came to a scene he'd seen clips and reimaginings of before: Leo takes Kate to the bow of the ship and asks her to trust him. He holds her hand, and she leans forward, over the waves, feeling free.

Alana paused the movie. "I remember this!"

Caleb was more caught up in the movie than he'd expected. Right, she'd remembered her mother talking about it.

"What do you remember?"

"Mom talked about this scene. My father did the pose with her, that night. On his car—they sat on the hood, and she stood on the bumper, and he held her up while she was the king of the world. They weren't the only ones doing it that night. Everyone was having fun. Then my dad, her husband...well, didn't die, but I think it was the last fun time they had together."

"You think she hid whatever at the place where they parked the car and did that pose?" Caleb could imagine a whole lot of digging if so.

Alana's face fell. "I'm not sure that's going to help. But I did remember something new. Maybe there's more in the movie that will trigger another memory."

Caleb mentally slapped himself. "I didn't mean to complain. It's great that you're remembering things. Any memory might be the one to tell us what we're looking for."

The happy look was gone, though. His fault.

"I'm glad, even if you don't remember something to pinpoint what spot your mother was thinking of, that you're still getting back some memories. And a happy one. Some things that are true, right? A chance to know your father."

She nodded slowly. "Yeah. I'll never get to really

know him, and all the details of what happened with my mom and dad and at the jewelry store, but I know now that he was willing to reenact that scene with Mom, and that must have been a good memory for her. A guy doing that has some redeeming qualities, right?"

Caleb wanted to have redeeming qualities, too. Before he quite realized, he said, "Hey, stand up for a minute."

Alana stood, waiting to see what he was going to do.

"Close your eyes."

He wasn't that subtle. She was holding back a smile. "Really?"

"Do you trust me?"

In response, Alana closed her eyes.

"Stand on the coffee table." Caleb held her hand to help her up, and turned her so that she was facing the TV, then stood behind her. The height differential didn't match the film, but he didn't care.

"Stretch out your arms."

Alana held them out and slightly back. Caleb moved behind her and tangled her fingers with his.

"Open your eyes."

Alana leaned forward. "I'm flying!"

He wanted her to fly, to feel confident and happy, every day. She turned to him, like Kate did to Leo. They stared into each other's eyes. If he'd been taller, or the table lower, he'd have been in the same position as Leo. They could have kissed. He was sure that she would have let him, that she wanted to.

A pang of guilt lanced through him. He couldn't, not until she knew who he was. Maybe he was more like the villainous boyfriend than the hero.

"So, do I have some redeeming qualities?" His voice

was low and rough. It wasn't the voice of someone joking.

"Definitely," she whispered. They were quiet, unsure what to say.

Rex sat up, and the moment was broken. Caleb stepped back, and Alana jumped down.

"Want to watch some more? I'm getting interested in this now."

"Sure. I'm getting a drink. Can I bring you something?"

"Water would be great." Caleb sat down and fussed with Rex. He wanted to tell Alana that he'd like to kiss her, more than almost anything, but he couldn't explain why he hadn't, not now. She wouldn't trust him, not if she knew he'd been lying to her, so much like her mother had, and if she didn't trust him, didn't keep him close, he couldn't protect her. He'd never felt worse about this assignment.

Alana returned with water for both of them. She sat down and restarted the movie.

It wasn't the same. Caleb was aware of every move Alana made, every sigh. It was hard to focus on the movie when she was stealing all his attention. When the ship finally hit the iceberg, his interest in the movie perked back up, though he was still aware of Alana. And when Jack froze in the water, he couldn't control his outburst.

"There was room for two people on that door!"

Alana laughed. "You're not the first person to argue that."

"They could have at least tried. That was…that was bad."

Alana paused the movie. "It's just a story. Leo, the actor, lived and did many more movies."

Caleb rolled his eyes. "I know. But the writers should have done better."

Alana stared at the paused TV. "Maybe they should have." She hit Play again, and the movie wound on to its conclusion.

The credits rolled. Caleb wanted to ask if anything had inspired more memories for Alana but didn't want to push her.

"That was your mother's favorite movie?"

Alana switched off the TV. "Actually, no. At least, not that I knew. She never watched it, not when I was around. The regular version has a more adult scene, but we could have watched this version if that was the only reason. I heard about the movie from other people and watched it at a friend's house, but it wasn't until I tried to remember her stories that I thought of it. I don't know if she hated it because of my father, or if it was too painful to think about."

The corners of Alana's mouth pulled down. Caleb knew this was another thing she'd never know about her parents. Another mystery.

Caleb couldn't tell her the answer to this question, but he was holding on to information about her family that he didn't share because he wasn't supposed to know it. When this ended, however it ended, she'd get the chance to know that expanded story, but he doubted he'd be the one to tell her.

She'd be upset with him, and he'd be moving on. He hated that thought. He didn't want to think about that now. "Did you like the movie?" he asked her.

"I couldn't get into it this time. I kept looking for

clues. I didn't see anything, and I've probably dragged you all the way here for nothing."

Not for nothing. And he'd been encouraging her all the way. She'd understand that, later. When she found out the truth about him.

"I know this has been a difficult few days for you. Lots of upheaval, life-changing revelations, someone after you—you've been handling it well. If it's getting to you now, that's understandable."

Alana ran her hands through her hair. "I want to be the kind of person who can just deal with it. When you and I are busy, and even when we think someone is after us, it's a distraction, you know? I have something to focus on. But right now, this, trying to remember about my mom and realizing I didn't know her—how am I supposed to figure out where she hid something? It's hopeless."

Caleb drew her into his arms, needing to offer her comfort.

"Shh. It's okay. You're doing the best you can."

Alana tucked her head under his chin. It felt like she'd been designed to fit in that spot perfectly.

"I don't know how I'd have gotten through this without you. You have been a godsend. Literally. I'd have been taken by those men, and not had a clue what they wanted. I don't know what they would have done to me."

That thought had him tightening his arms, unwilling to consider those possibilities. He wanted to tell her he wasn't a godsend, but rather sent by the RCMP. But maybe God had used Yoxall to send him here to care for Alana and keep her safe.

He wanted his cover story to be real. To be honest

about who he was and have a future back in Winnipeg
with her. But at least his cover had made it possible for
him to protect her.

So he tucked his chin on her hair and rubbed circles
on her back. He felt her muscles ease as the tension
leached away. He wasn't her future. But he could take
care of her in the present, and that would have to do.

Chapter Eighteen

Alana didn't want to move. It felt so good, being held in Caleb's strong arms.

This experience, being thrown into a new frame of knowledge, being in danger, wasn't something she'd asked for. She hadn't been given a choice, but she was dealing with it, and learning about herself. Learning that she could handle danger and stress, and that when she couldn't, she could lean on someone else.

She didn't know what would happen once they tried to find this thing her mother had hidden. They might find it, though the odds of that were slim. They might have to give up without any success. They might be found by the people who were also after it, and for that she had to trust God would protect them.

But when it was over, they could go back to Winnipeg and Caleb would finally get to work on his research. He'd be next door. Affection, attraction…she wanted more with him. She thought he did, too. She wouldn't say anything, not now, not when she'd cause him discomfort if she were wrong. But surely, this— the way he was giving her comfort—meant something.

She broke his embrace reluctantly. They needed to get some rest to resume their efforts tomorrow. Alana would happily fall asleep in Caleb's arms, but it wouldn't be comfortable for him. They weren't at that stage yet, but she hoped they would be.

"Thank you, Caleb. I needed that."

A corner of his mouth quirked up. "I think I did, too."

She drew in a breath. "So, we'll have a good rest tonight, and tomorrow check out the other drive-ins and make a plan, right?"

"Right."

"I'm going to think positive. We'll find this, somehow."

"We will. I believe it."

She looked down. "Plus, we have Rex helping. And God. We're an unbeatable team."

Caleb tucked a strand of hair behind her ear. "You're a great teammate."

"You are, too."

That was all they could say, but the compliment warmed her. She made her way to one of the bedrooms—they'd found a place with two bedrooms this time and Caleb thought it was secure enough to sleep separately—and prepared for bed. She prayed, asking God for guidance, and thanking Him for her teammates, Caleb and Rex.

She thought she'd toss and turn, trying to figure things out, but when her head hit the pillow, she fell into a deep sleep. When she woke up, she knew what to do.

She wanted to blurt it out as soon as she left the bedroom, but Caleb was in his own room, still sleeping, judging from the lack of sounds. Rex waited by the door, but Alana wasn't going to risk upsetting Caleb again.

"Sorry, Rex." The dog lay down, nose on his paws, a disgruntled expression on his face.

Alana started the coffee maker. Either she wasn't as quiet as she hoped, or the smell of coffee was potent, because Caleb soon appeared in the doorway of his room.

"Good morning!" Alana was almost unbearably perky for this early in the day, but she felt optimistic that she finally understood what her mother had done. That and her hopes for a future with Caleb had sent her mood soaring.

"You're up early."

Alana turned to Caleb. "I think I've figured it out." Caleb's eyes opened wide. "But first Rex needs to go out, so you can watch over us while I take him into the backyard."

Caleb followed her to the door, and into the yard.

"I'm dying to hear what you came up with."

Alana grinned. "Someone was still getting his beauty sleep when I got up, so he'll have to wait for Rex."

Rex took his time, checking out every bush and tree carefully before making his selection. He didn't find anything to catch his attention, and Caleb didn't, either. Once Rex was done, they went back into their rental.

"So, what did you come up with?"

"Coffee?" Alana held up the pot.

"Coffee can wait."

Alana poured two cups full. "Coffee can be drunk while you listen."

Caleb sat at the small table, while Alana leaned

against the countertop. "I'm going to ignore the two bigger theaters. I may not remember Mom's words exactly, but I got the impression that there was only one movie option. And since those two are still in use, they'd be more difficult to check out, right?"

"We can start with the abandoned ones, and if we need to get to the active theaters, we'll have to ask for help."

"I also don't know how far some teenagers would be allowed to go on their own at one of those places. Since their last date was the same place as their first date, I don't think it's far from Barrie. I think we should start with the creepy deserted theater that's the second closest."

Caleb's brow creased. "Okay, we can start with that. But there's still a lot of ground to cover."

"I'm pretty sure I can narrow it down."

His eyes narrowed. "You remembered something?"

Alana shook her head. "No, nothing that my mom told me, but I thought about the movie. Or my brain did while I was sleeping."

"The part where the two of them stand at the front of the boat?"

Her cheeks flushed. "No. Um, there's that big diamond in the film, right?"

Caleb sat upright. "Yeah. The one she drops in the ocean."

"Exactly. And my mom was thinking of that movie, she must have been, when she was considering where to hide this thing. She didn't like the movie they saw the first time they were at the drive-in, so that wouldn't have been on her mind the same way. If you take the movie *Titanic* and the place she saw it and add that she had something valuable to hide…"

Caleb's head tilted. "So she…dropped it in the lake? Is there a lake nearby?"

"I think she buried it below the movie screen."

It had been as clear as day to Alana when she woke up. She pictured the actress in the movie, dropping the diamond over the side of the boat. And saw her mother hiding whatever her valuable was where she'd seen the diamond drop. Off the movie screen, onto the ground below.

Now she was afraid she sounded like an idiot.

Caleb's forehead creases deepened as he considered. She wanted to backtrack, unsure of herself, but what else did they have to go on?

"Would she have done that?" He didn't sound as skeptical as she'd feared.

"Maybe? It made perfect sense when I woke up."

Caleb's fingers tapped on the table. "We'll need shovels then."

Alana almost sagged against the counter. He was willing to try.

"I can pull up that scene again, try to figure out roughly where that might be in relation to the movie screen."

Caleb swallowed his coffee in one go. He looked like his mind was racing. "It makes a kind of sense, doesn't it? It's worth a try at least. I don't think anyone will care if we dig something up there."

He thought her idea was possible, at least. "So, should we pack up and go?"

Caleb headed to his room. "Why don't you and Rex wait here while I pick up some fresh coffee and get a couple of shovels, maybe a tarp…and work gloves? Bug spray, too."

Alana heard him grabbing the keys for the SUV. She felt deflated. Like he was leaving her behind. He wouldn't just go find this thing and leave her, would he? Prickles moved up her spine.

Caleb came back out, heading for the door.

"Hey, Caleb."

He looked back, body still tilted forward like he couldn't wait to leave.

"You're not going out there on your own, are you?"

That made him turn back, cross to her. He put a hand on her cheek.

"I'm not abandoning you, I swear. But we're close, and I'm nervous that whoever is after us might see you and follow us, so I don't want to have you waiting in the truck while I get the stuff we need, and I don't want to leave Rex in the car on his own. Not sure he'd be welcome inside the store. I'll be back for you with the equipment. You try to narrow down the area we're going to dig in, and don't let anyone in."

She nodded but wasn't completely reassured. Was Caleb hiding something from her?

Caleb called Yoxall from the parking lot of the nearest hardware store, as soon as the SUV was turned off.

"Alana thinks she's figured it out."

"Good work." Yoxall's praise was good to hear, but it wasn't his work.

"It was all Alana. She remembered what movie her parents watched when they were last at the drive-in and took it from there. We're going to try the Elmvale Drive-In, since it's the closest single-screen theater. It's abandoned, so we can be there without attracting any attention. Can you make sure we're covered if someone comes by and calls us in for trespassing?"

"I can do that."

"From something in the movie, she thinks her mom might have hidden it under the screen."

"Hmm…" Caleb waited while Yoxall considered the information.

"If Fowler is tracking us still, is there someone we can ask for help, safely?"

"Give me a moment."

Yoxall put the phone on hold, and Caleb watched shoppers heading into the big-box hardware store. He reined in his impatience. He wanted this done, and Alana safe. Then he wanted to be honest with Alana. He wasn't sure what he hoped for with her, but he wanted something. He didn't want to be part of her past, never seen again.

"Caleb!"

"Yes, sir."

"We need you to do a couple of things."

"Of course."

"We need time to get some people out there, get some equipment set up, and then find a place to hide out while you two dig for this evidence. I'm going to reach out to some off-duty OPP officers I know."

Excellent. They wouldn't be on their own.

"And we need to get you seen."

Caleb felt like he'd swallowed ice. "What?"

That didn't make sense. If they were seen…sure, with Yoxall setting up people around them, they weren't going to be alone, but if Fowler and his crony found Alana and Caleb at the theater, things could happen before the backup arrived. He would take that risk for himself, but not for Alana.

Yoxall continued. "I don't know what evidence Campbell might have hidden, or his wife hid again. We can hope it's the missing security tape and jewelry, but it's more than possible that the tape would be ruined by this point in time, and unless the jewelry has fingerprints, it's not going to tie anyone else to the crime.

"But if someone comes after you, and we can charge them for attempted kidnapping, burglary, assault and anything else they might do when they find you, then we've got a chance to make some charges stick."

Caleb's thoughts swirled. The chance of finding the hidden evidence—it had always been a long shot. But Yoxall had approved of them driving east, risking an interaction with Fowler…

"You knew this from the beginning—that the evidence might be useless."

"Of course I did."

"You didn't tell me."

"I didn't know what was going to play out. It was better that you didn't know more than you did, better for your cover."

Caleb wanted to know all the facts before trying something like this, but that argument wouldn't get him anywhere. Undercover, you couldn't accidentally tell something you didn't know. It was a kind of protection. But risking Alana wasn't something he could agree to.

"Why don't I leave Alana behind? We don't need her, do we?"

"I don't think you're going to be followed unless she's there. And you might need her. Maybe she'll think of something else in case this spot doesn't pan out."

Caleb had promised he wouldn't leave her behind. "She'll be at risk."

"She's been at risk since this started. What if they found where you hid her or track her down while you're out digging at the theater? At least you have your gun and the dog. You'll have to protect her."

And he would. He listened while Yoxall told him how long to delay, and where he needed to travel so that they'd be followed to the Elmvale Drive-In.

Caleb didn't like it at all.

Chapter Nineteen

Alana wasn't sure why she was feeling so unsettled. Or more accurately, she didn't know which of the many possibilities was the main cause.

This morning Caleb had seemed…shifty somehow. After being so adamant that he was always with her to protect her, he'd left her alone twice. He'd been gone a long time and hadn't reached out until he was on his way back. She was trusting him with a lot. And despite her feelings, which insisted he was trustworthy and that she liked him…and maybe more than liked him, she had only known him a matter of days. Very intense, emotional days that they'd spent almost constantly in each other's company. She was placing a lot of faith in her instincts, his dog and Mr. Conners's recommendation.

When Caleb was gone, and she only had her thoughts and Rex for company, questions troubled her. Why did Caleb have a highly trained dog and not know anything about the dog or the great-uncle who left Rex to him? He'd been with her nonstop since he arrived. Was that because he liked her company and wanted to protect her, or was his interest solely in what they were looking for? Had he somehow known about it, and befriended her on purpose? Was she being played?

There was this whole "secret life my mother hid from me" issue as well. There was a lot to deal with, and she hadn't had the time to consider all the ramifications that followed, tumbling down like dominoes. The break-ins, the abduction, the damage to the vehicle. Now she was planning to dig on someone else's property to uncover evidence of a crime her father had served time for. Why hadn't her mother prepared her?

Maybe she should call the police, the OPP here, and leave it to them. Maybe that meant a dirty cop would get away with something. Maybe there wasn't a dirty cop, and nothing to find. Otherwise, all she could do was pray, and hope that her trust in Caleb wasn't a mistake.

No, prayer shouldn't be her last-ditch response. She'd allowed her time with God to slip away since this had all started. She needed, when she was unsettled and uncomfortable, to make that a priority. She would pray and ask her heavenly Father for guidance, whether to trust Caleb, or call the police.

Caleb was anxious about Alana, so the wait lasted forever. He was afraid she'd worry, might think he'd been attacked or intercepted, or even that he'd gone without her. He wanted to send her a quick text to reassure her that he hadn't flaked on her, and make sure she was okay, but he didn't know when he was returning. He needed an excuse that would fit the time frame he'd be returning in.

He'd found the equipment they needed to dig, and

stored it in the back seat. There was nothing more to do except stare at his phone, willing Yoxall to give him the okay to get going. He had a few email messages that he mostly ignored, but he made note of the one with the training information for Rex. At least Yoxall had found that. Finally, he got the thumbs-up from Yoxall, and could text Alana to reassure her.

Sorry, had to go to more than one store.

She sent back a thumbs-up, which didn't give enough information. Was she anxious, angry or suspicious? He went to a drive-through for coffee and rushed back to the rental as soon as he could. He'd still been longer than he'd intended, and longer than he liked. He needed to see her, make sure she was safe.

Before he exposed her to more danger.

Alana opened the door to his knock. "I need that coffee." There was something different about her, something guarded in her smile. Had his delay in returning eaten away at the trust they'd shared?

"Sorry it took so long—like I texted, I had to try a couple of stores to find everything." He passed her the coffee and shut the door behind him. "Are you okay?"

Alana nodded. "I packed up the few things we brought, so we're ready anytime."

"No one came by?"

"Our host stopped to make sure we found everything we needed. Rex wasn't welcoming, but I told them we were fine."

"Okay. Shall we get on our way?"

Caleb was anxious to get this over with, now that they would be deliberately courting danger. Adrenaline had been spiking through him since he'd talked to Yoxall, and he needed to do something.

Alana didn't show any outward signs of worry as she carried her bag to the SUV, so Caleb had to accept that he was probably the one who was acting differently. Since Caleb had stored his purchases in the back seat, they put Rex in the back again. Once they were all in the vehicle, Caleb pulled up his phone and found the message about Rex. He opened the attachment and passed the phone to her.

"I just got the information on Rex. Maybe you could check that out while we drive."

Alana nodded and focused on what was showing on the phone, slight furrows between her brows as she read. He wanted to smooth those away with his fingers, but instead, he put the SUV in gear and headed out.

He'd noted the route Yoxall wanted them to take and followed the directions. He couldn't prevent himself from watching, wondering where Fowler might be, and if he was following them again. Alana looked up once, frowning.

"Is this downtown?"

"I messed up the directions." The lie tasted sour in his mouth, but Alana didn't call him on it.

She looked around them. "No one is following?"

He shook his head. Maybe their would-be abductor and thief wasn't anywhere on this route, or maybe he didn't recognize them—they might have switched vehicles as well. Yoxall's information could be faulty. Fowler might still be searching somewhere else, and they'd be perfectly safe out at the drive-in. They might not find enough information to put the guy away, but Alana would be out of danger. There'd be other routes they could pursue to get this guy—there had to be. Caleb doubted this incident with Campbell was the only time he'd crossed the line.

He wanted to call the whole thing off, but he kept driving. They were out of the city of Barrie, on the short drive to Elmvale, when Alana spoke. "Caleb, Rex is trained in apprehension and subduing people."

Caleb tightened his grip on the steering wheel. "I didn't get much information about him."

Alana huffed a breath. "He's a highly trained animal. Trained to be a weapon. They don't let just anyone have these dogs. How did your great-uncle get him, and give him to you without some kind of requirements?"

Caleb didn't have the bandwidth to think about the dog right now. They had bigger things to worry about, but he couldn't tell Alana that.

"My uncle used to be a dog trainer, but I thought it was simple obedience. Maybe it was more than that and no one told me. Do you think he'll obey you with what you've learned in the email?"

Alana threw up her hands. "*You* need to be able to control him. He's your dog."

Caleb drew a breath. Everything she was saying was right, but so many things about this whole assignment had gone off track. He hadn't been given proper information about the dog. This road trip wasn't planned for. And his feelings about Alana...

But he shouldn't take out his frustration and fears on her.

"I know. I'm sorry. I'll make sure I learn everything I need to, but I'm thinking more about what we're about to do once we get to Elmvale than about Rex right now. You probably will understand it better than me, since you've had a dog. Once we're done, you can tell me what you've figured out, and I'll work with him. I'll try to find out how my great-uncle got him."

"You're nervous, aren't you?" Alana looked behind them. "Anyone following?"

Caleb shook his head.

"Then all we're going to do is dig up some dirt, and probably not find anything. But you need to take your adoption of Rex seriously."

"I will. I promise."

He wanted to claw those words back. He couldn't make promises to Alana, especially not promises like that. Rex would go back to his owner, once the man recovered. The dog was not going to be in Caleb's life, but then again, neither was Alana. She'd never know if he'd kept his promise or not.

It was a relief to see the tattered screen of the drive-in ahead of them.

"There it is."

Alana shut down the phone and leaned forward. "It's still creepy."

"I won't argue with you about that."

She rubbed her hands on her shorts. "I don't know if I want to find out I'm right or not."

That startled him. "Don't you want this to be over? To get your life back?"

"Yes. Not to be worried that someone is following me, or going to sabotage my car, or break into my house or come after me. But even if this is right, if we find whatever my mother hid here today, I won't have my life back. Not the same life."

Caleb wanted to touch her, try to comfort her, but she

twisted in her seat, staring through the window, blocking him out. Was that deliberate?

"But you'll be safe."

She shrugged. "I'll be safe from one specific, targeted danger. I won't be safe from car accidents or cancer or any of the things people live with every day. I'll have to come to terms with the fact that my mother lied to me, and that I'm not the person I thought I was."

She was thinking too much about her parents, and not concentrating on the wonderful person she was. "You're the same person, just with a different backstory."

"Backstory matters. And I know I'll get through it. I have friends, and I have God. But it's not going to be easy. And I have questions I know I'll never have the answers to."

"Alana…"

She waved a hand. "Don't mind me. Just weird thoughts. We need to focus on this."

They drove in past the overgrown grass by the ticket booth, and around the back of the screen to face the parking area. Caleb drove a tight circle and pulled up close to the front of the screen.

"No one will see us from the road."

Alana nodded. "Let's do this."

Chapter Twenty

Caleb had brought his purchases from the hardware store out of the SUV, set them in front of the vehicle, and was ready to begin. But Alana wasn't ready. Not yet.

Standing beside the vehicle, she looked up at the big, ragged screen that had shown the movies people had enjoyed over the years. When it was built, it must have been impressive, daunting from this close. But it was a man-made object, and it was failing.

She had to trust someone who wouldn't fail.

Caleb pulled out one of the new pairs of gloves he'd bought and passed her another pair.

"Thank you." She met his gaze, chin raised. "I need a moment before we begin."

His brow furrowed and his mouth started to open, but he snapped his jaw shut.

"I'm going to pray. I need that grounding before we do anything else."

He was so on edge she expected him to react and remind her they didn't have a lot of time. Instead, his head dropped.

"You're right, Alana. I should have remembered that myself. Guidance?"

She nodded. "But not for the place to dig. For His will to be done. Whatever it is."

She bowed her head. She didn't want to pray out loud. This was a quick unloading of her fears, her worries, and handing them over. It wasn't long, but she felt peace gentle her anxious mind.

It didn't matter if Caleb had secrets, or if there was someone after her. It didn't matter if she found this or not. What mattered was that God's will be done. She could do that, as He led her step by step.

A last moment of calm, and then she opened her eyes. Caleb started to smile at her as they shared a moment of peace together. Then there was the sound of a vehicle coming into the drive-in, fast, and Alana glanced toward the entrance, and back to Caleb. He was watchful and wary, but not surprised. She had only a moment to consider that before a black SUV turned the corner and accelerated directly at them.

Alana and Caleb leaped out of the way and ended up each on one side of the vehicle as it braked to an abrupt halt. A man shoved open the door, gun in hand. Alana froze.

"Stop right there." A stranger's voice from the other side of the vehicle indicated that the same thing was happening on Caleb's side. Alana's pulse quickened, and her breathing sped up.

"Where's the dog?" the man holding the gun on her asked. Alana was standing beside their rented SUV, and Rex was in the back. Should she pretend she didn't know?

"I can shoot your vehicle. See if he's in there."

Alana swallowed. "Rex is in the back."

"Bring him out, nice and slow. Any sudden moves, and I'm shooting the dog."

Alana glanced at the man's face. He looked completely comfortable with the idea of hurting an animal. Maybe this was the man Rex had tackled back in Winnipeg.

"I'll be careful." She moved slowly to the back and opened the hatch, hand up to keep Rex from jumping out. Should she try one of the commands she'd read in that file Caleb had shared with her?

No. Rex had been hurt safeguarding her. She had to protect him now. She grabbed his lead and gently tugged. The dog hopped down and turned to stare at the man behind her. The threat he'd been trained to deal with. Rex's hackles rose, and a growl sounded in his chest.

Not now, Rex.

She lifted a hand to close the hatch, but the rough voice said, "No."

Footsteps, and Caleb and the other man came around the back of the stranger's SUV. Caleb came first, hands raised, the other man directing his revolver at Caleb's back.

"Get together, both of you and the dog."

Caleb moved to stand beside her.

"Turn around, hands on the vehicle. Legs spread."

Like something from a TV show or movie. Caleb nodded when she glanced at him, and she did as they'd asked. Rough hands moved over her, and she repressed a shudder. Then they moved to Caleb. Rex beside her was vibrating with his need to act. She hoped his training held, because if he moved, he'd be shot.

"Any more weapons?"

They must have found Caleb's gun.

"No," Caleb answered, but the sounds of hands slapping on clothing indicated they didn't believe him.

"That's all they have on them."

"Search the vehicle."

While Alana stared at the paint on the SUV before her, she heard the sounds of their belongings being thrown on the ground.

"No weapons. Nothing useful."

The man moved back behind them.

"Turn around. Slowly."

Alana did as he asked, and Caleb did the same beside her. She let her hand rest on Rex's head, restraining and calming the dog.

"Looks like the two of you came here to do some digging. Don't let us stop you."

"What do you want?" Caleb asked the question quietly, but he didn't sound as upset or as frightened as Alana would have expected.

The man who'd been driving smiled. It wasn't a nice smile.

"I want the same thing you two want. So, you're gonna dig for it, and I'm going to take it."

Chapter Twenty-One

There were no more questions about whether the threat was real, and if Alana's mother had hidden something incriminating. Alana wanted to ask these men whether they'd let her and Caleb go if they did what the men asked and gave them what they wanted. But the strangers weren't hiding, weren't doing anything to disguise themselves. They weren't worried that she and Caleb might go to the police and press charges. She expected that her and Caleb's bodies would end up filling the holes they dug to try to find the missing evidence. Rex as well.

There was a good chance they were going to die here.

She searched for the peace she'd felt earlier, when she'd decided to trust the path Caleb had brought them on rather than calling the OPP. She pushed past her fear and felt the calm. She was ready. She didn't want to die—she hadn't quite got to the point Paul had in his epistle, but she was confident about what came after. She thought Caleb was, too. She had no decisions to make, except to follow any leading she got from God, or from Caleb. Because while she might not fear death, she'd like to stop these men. The world would be better if they weren't free to do what they wished.

She had no offensive skills to try to overcome them. She wouldn't risk Caleb or Rex. She just had to trust God and see what happened. Even if it weren't the outcome she'd choose on her own.

Why not find out what was going on? Maybe get some answers to the questions she had. Since they didn't plan to let them go, she could at least satisfy her curiosity.

"What are you looking for, and why?"

Caleb flinched beside her. Maybe she shouldn't have spoken.

The man who appeared to be in charge and giving the orders frowned at her. "You don't know? You're digging here, and you don't know why?"

Alana shook her head. "All I had to go on were those letters you stole."

He huffed a disbelieving laugh. "Your mother didn't tell you? That wasn't just a story you made up for this guy?"

They'd been listening. "I knew nothing until I opened that safety deposit box."

The man shook his head. "Never would have guessed Marie didn't tell you. But if that's the case, how come you're here?"

"Tell me your story, and I'll tell you mine."

He raised an eyebrow. "I can just shoot the dog and your boyfriend here until you tell me anyway."

"My story doesn't really matter, if I'm right that this is where Mom hid whatever it is."

He considered her for a moment. "True. How much do you know about your parents?"

"Their real story, or what my mother told me?"

"I underestimated Marie. The real story. I don't care what she told you to cover it up."

"I only know what I could find in the newspaper clippings and on the internet. My dad was a jeweler, and he broke the law by fencing stolen goods. He and another man, a cop, decided to steal from the insurance company by faking a robbery. The cop died, and my dad went to jail."

"Your mother testified. Against your father."

Was he telling her that to upset her? He had a cruel look to his face. "She claimed there was another cop involved. I assume that's why we were in witness protection."

The man grinned. "Marie was a sharp one. Yes, there was another cop involved. Named Fowler, and since right now it's important that his image be squeaky clean, I need to find what your mother hid and destroy it."

Caleb was silent beside her. She didn't know why. But she was willing to ask questions. This man, presumably Fowler, wanted to talk. Maybe to brag about how clever he was. Perhaps that was why Caleb was quiet—he probably thought if they didn't know anything, they'd have a better chance of getting away.

"What she hid must be proof that you were involved. You're going to kill us anyway, so why not admit who you are?"

"Marie's daughter is also clever. Yes. I was the brains of the whole plan. It was almost foolproof."

He still sounded bitter.

"What went wrong?"

"Your father got cold feet. Decided he didn't want to

go through with it. I have no idea where that fit of con-
science came from. The man was a fence, so it wasn't
like he was innocent."

No, he wasn't innocent, but he'd at least had a change
of heart about this one thing. Alana was happy to know
he'd taken a stand. "Then what happened? Did you try
to make him participate?"

"I tried to shut his mouth. He wasn't going to hold
that over me for the rest of my life. I could have taken
him in for possession of stolen goods. He'd have
served time, but he could have fingered me. Nothing
that would stick, but people would start watching me.
Then that idiot Abbott got in the middle."

Alana gasped. "My dad didn't shoot at him?"

"Your father didn't have the guts. It was an accident,
since Abbott fell back on a display case and broke his
skull, but I wasn't going to go down for that or the con-
spiracy charges. I told your father if he even thought
about implicating me, he should consider what would
happen to you and your mother."

Alana blinked. "He didn't do it, but he didn't say
anything?"

"Because he was only partially a fool. He knew I
would follow through. My father was one of the top
cops in the province. I wasn't going down without making someone pay."

Alana shivered. The malevolence came off the man
in waves. But he shifted on his feet, as if he were ready
to move on, and she didn't want to miss the chance to
get as much information as she could.

"What did my father and mother hide? If you were
untouchable, what did it matter?"

His brows drew down, and he scowled.

"Apparently there was a security tape. Your father had it set up in the store. I didn't know until Marie told me, but it could…it could have recorded the entire incident. She claimed it did."

Alana's hands gripped tightly in Rex's ruff. "If Mom and Dad had proof, why didn't they just expose you?"

"My father and I have a lot of influence. Evidence may go missing, and then, poof! No case, but they knew I'd make them pay. I didn't need other cops watching everything I did. If they kept quiet, then I agreed to leave all of you alone."

"And once my father was safely imprisoned? You didn't know where Mom and I went. How did you find me?"

He snorted. "I always knew where you were. I told you, my father can find out anything. Your mother said she'd done something with the tape, and if either of you died, then it would go to the press."

That threat had worked, and had kept them safe, until her mother died. But she hadn't set up anything to happen after her death. She'd hidden the evidence instead. Trying to forget it happened? Didn't trust anyone else? So when nothing happened…

"You were expecting the information to come out after she passed."

The man tapped his fingers on the gun, but his gaze remained sharply focused on her. "It seems your mother didn't trust anyone. I waited, after she died. Waited for that bomb to go off. But nothing. Bullet dodged. Except, that evidence still exists.

"My father is running for office. This is a loose end that needs to be tied up. Once there's no risk of anything coming out at an awkward time, we're all set. Any more questions?"

There were, Alana was sure. But she couldn't think of them right now.

"So, now your story. Or I can have Fred shoot one of the dog's legs."

Alana moved in front of the dog. "There's not much to tell. You saw those letters—you're the one who stole them, aren't you?"

A growl. "Thought that package would have included the tape, but no. Just maudlin letters from your father and a vague letter of your mother's."

What had happened to the letters they'd taken? If they hadn't been destroyed yet, they would be, as soon as this man got the evidence against him. Alana kept talking, keeping her part of the bargain.

"I wasn't sure she'd told me the truth, but she'd said her last date with my father was at a drive-in movie theater."

The man looked around. "This one?"

"I think so. I'm going on what I remember of stories she told me. I think it was a small drive-in, it was near Barrie, and the movie they saw was *Titanic*."

"She buried it somewhere here."

Alana looked toward the screen. "Yes. Where the older Rose in the movie would have appeared to drop the diamond. In this case, it isn't in the Atlantic. But over there, under the screen."

Caleb kept quiet with an effort. He didn't want Alana to have anything to do with Fowler. He'd recognized the man from the information Yoxall had given him. Caleb would be panicking, if he hadn't known Yoxall had his men nearby, watching and waiting for their moment.

Now would be a good time.

Alana had unknowingly been perfect, getting Fowler to tell the whole story in return for her cooperation in sharing where she thought the evidence was hidden. He'd had nothing to do but stand back and let Fowler expose himself. But it was time for the cavalry to show up. Before Fowler dug up the evidence that might support the case against him. Dug it up and destroyed it.

Giving that confession proved he had no intentions of leaving them alive to testify against him. Caleb had known that there was danger, especially to Alana, but he hadn't appreciated just how far Fowler was willing to go to maintain his secrets.

Long breaths. Yoxall would show up anytime. The sooner the better.

Fowler smiled. "Thank you for making that easier for your boyfriend. I was afraid I'd have to start hurting him before I knew where to make him dig."

"You're going to make us do the work, and then what, kill us?" Alana was still fearless. Didn't she understand the danger?

Fowler laughed. "Are you going to promise not to tell anyone?"

Alana shook her head. "You wouldn't believe us. But if you're going to kill us anyway, why should we do anything to help you?"

"I can make the dog suffer if you don't cooperate."

Alana sucked in a breath.

"You're a veterinarian. Probably would do almost anything so I don't hurt that dog, right? I'd offer to shoot him—" his head jerked toward Caleb "—but I need him to dig. Still, I could find some way to hurt him without making it impossible for him to handle the shovel."

Caleb kept his head still but surreptitiously scanned the perimeter the best he could, looking for the promised support.

"And if he still won't dig, I'll have to hurt you. But in case you're wrong about this place, and might have more ideas, I don't want to kill you."

"Yet." Alana's voice was still strong.

"Yet." The guns never wavered. "This is probably a good time to let your boyfriend know that his friends aren't coming. Just in case he had any ideas about reinforcements arriving."

Caleb froze. Alana frowned. "Friends?"

"He thinks some cops are coming. Oh, he's been careful, but word got out about what he and Yoxall were up to. The RCMP don't have jurisdiction here, but Yoxall has contacts in the OPP. Those off-duty officers who were supposed to have this place covered, discreetly, were just called in for a school shooting drill about twenty minutes ago. Worst-case scenario, with several schools involved, so it's all hands on deck. It was the best idea Dad could come up with on short notice."

"What?" Caleb couldn't stay still. "You can't suddenly trigger a shooting drill."

Fowler rolled his eyes. "My father dropped a word in the right ear. With all the shooting events that happen in the United States, a surprise drill was in order. To make it realistic, no one will be notified that it's only a drill for a while yet, and there's going to be *so* much paperwork to fill out to evaluate the team responses.

Should give us plenty of time here before anyone is free to check this place out."

He jerked his head toward the screen.

"Time to dig."

Chapter Twenty-Two

Caleb's hands flexed into fists. Alana was staring at him in shock, and his mind raced. How was he going to get them out of this with no backup?

Yoxall would do something, send someone, but he didn't know when. Not until everything was worked out with the shooting drill, or until he could bring in people from somewhere else. Would he guess that the drill was a deliberate distraction, and not an unfortunate coincidence?

There might not be enough time. Fowler had something planned.

"Move, Mountie. Go pick up a shovel, carefully. You try to throw it, swing it at us, or anything other than walking to the base of that screen and starting to dig, I shoot the dog first."

Caleb raised his hands and took careful steps toward the shovel.

"Mountie?" Alana's voice expressed her confusion.

"Oh, he didn't tell you? What was this, an undercover mission? Yes, your boyfriend there is a cop, trying to get evidence for his boss. I didn't know, either, until yesterday. Maybe he could have had a future with that. It worked for me. Lying, cheating…almost anything goes when you're undercover, right? The end justifies the means."

Caleb risked a glance at Alana. She was watching him, mouth soft and sad. Then her eyes narrowed, and her expression blanked. Something twinged in his chest. He'd known this would hurt her, leave her feeling betrayed, but he could explain. It was his job, he was protecting her…but all the reasonings fell flat.

"Move!" Fowler was losing patience.

Caleb picked up the shovel and walked to the screen.

"Where's the spot—what's the name now—Alana?"

Caleb looked at her, but she wouldn't meet his gaze.

"About two feet to the right."

Caleb clenched his jaw and moved over two feet. He pushed the shovel in and pressed down. Tilted the handle back, lifted the dirt and threw it aside.

Then he did it again. And again.

The whole time he dug, he considered and discarded possibilities, a way to overcome Fowler and his helper without getting Alana or Rex hurt. His gaze moved from the dirt in front of him to the staged tableau by the SUVs.

Fowler asked Alana about her mother, but Alana didn't answer. Fowler shrugged. Caleb paused with the shovel in the ground, glancing sideways. There had to be a moment when he'd have his chance to do *something*.

Fowler's henchman, Fred, didn't speak. He simply kept his weapon aimed at Caleb, making sure he didn't step out of line. The man leaned against the hood of their SUV, occasionally changing pistol hands. Could he shoot well with his less dominant hand? They were at close range. Chances were he could shoot well enough.

Even if he didn't hit Caleb, Fowler had a gun trained where Alana was pressed against Rex. Alana's arms were crossed, and her gaze stayed on the ground. Caleb ached to reassure her, promise her he'd take care of this. Rex was sitting where Alana had commanded him, eyes on Fowler.

If Caleb were Fowler, he'd be nervous about that.

Caleb's muscles began to ache. He'd dug about three feet down at the original place Alana had indicated, and found nothing, so he moved on, expanding the trench he was creating on both ends.

He didn't know if Alana had identified the spot she really believed was where her mother would have buried the evidence, or had thought to misdirect Fowler. Caleb couldn't wait forever, though. Before he exhausted himself, he had to make a move.

He'd have one moment. When he found something, when his shovel hit something other than dirt, it would distract Fowler and his partner. Caleb would have to take his chance then. If Caleb moved, and Alana took advantage of the distraction to hide, he might be able to disable one person, acquire one weapon. There was no guarantee he'd find anything, and Caleb wasn't going to wait indefinitely. He'd make the moment if he needed to.

He glanced around again, using his peripheral vision. Fowler's muscle looked bored, but also alert enough. Fowler was beginning to fidget. He wouldn't wait much longer to do something—order a change in location for Caleb, threaten Alana for a different idea, or just give up and shoot the two of them. Caleb paused long enough to wipe the sweat off his brow.

"Keep going, Mountie."

Caleb hoped to catch Alana's eye, let her know he was going to make a move, but she was still staring at the ground. Okay, he had to do this on his own and pray she caught on. His mind threw up pleas to God while he prepared. He'd give it five more minutes...

Then his shovel hit something hard and clanged. The moment seemed to suspend forever. Caleb thought he caught a glimpse of rusty metal, but he didn't have time to look. Instead, he took a step back, eyes moving from Fred to Fowler to Alana. All three were looking at the trench. Then, things happened quickly.

Caleb pushed toward Fred, shovel up as a shield and potential weapon. Fowler took a step toward the ditch, and Alana said, "Go ahead, Rex."

Caleb must have caught Fred while his weaker hand held the gun. There was a retort, close enough to make Caleb's ears ring, but he ignored it. Then Caleb was near enough to swing the shovel. He caught the man's gun arm, the *thwack* sounding vicious as it made contact. The gun flew through the air, and Fred's other hand moved to cradle his wounded arm.

Caleb swung the shovel back at the man's legs, and he went down, hard. Caleb threw himself over the man, holding him down with his weight. The shovel fell beside him. He sat up, looking for the gun and to see what had happened to Fowler.

Fowler was on the ground, Rex's paws on his chest. The dog's jaws were open and that close to the man's vulnerable neck. Fowler's hands were spread beside him, his gun several feet away.

Alana stared, wide-eyed.

"Alana." She jerked and looked at him for the first time since Fowler had called him a Mountie.

"Can you grab the guns?"

She blinked, and he wondered if she'd understood him, or if the shock of the moment had incapacitated her. Then she moved, kicking the gun away from Fowler before she reached down to pick it up. Holding it gingerly, she came and grabbed Fred's. She held them out to Caleb, and he relaxed as that threat was mitigated.

Her eyes widened. "You're bleeding."

The adrenaline faded, and he felt a burning on his arm. He looked, and saw a scorch mark over his shirtsleeve, with blood beginning to seep out. He moved his arm—no pain beyond the surface level.

"It's just a scratch." He sat up, knees on Fred's chest and good arm. The man's face was ashen, and a sheen of sweat shone on his brow. Caleb had done real injury to his arm. His stomach churned. He didn't enjoy dealing out pain.

"Would you look in the cars, find something to use to tie these two up?"

Fred's eyes flickered, but he stayed mum.

"Can you call off your dog?" Fowler tried to sound forceful, but there was a current of fear underneath the words. Rex growled. Caleb and Alana ignored Fowler.

Alana returned with Rex's leash. Caleb tied Fred's good hand with one end and the other around his ankles, feet bent toward his back. He rolled the man so that he rested on his good arm.

A pained sound came out of the man's mouth. Caleb made sure there was no indication that the arm or anything else was serious enough to cause fatal or permanent damage.

Alana found some rope in the back of Fowler's SUV. On Alana's command, Rex moved off the man's chest, jaws still at Fowler's neck. Caleb pulled Fowler's wrists behind him and bound them tightly, before asking Alana to tell Rex to step back. Once Rex was a foot away from Fowler, giving Caleb room while still close enough to attack in a moment, Caleb was able to bind Fowler's hands to his ankles, same as Fred, and left him on his side.

Caleb found his phone, thrown on the ground when Fred had tossed through their possessions. There were alerts and messages from Yoxall, most of which had come through when they dropped coverage on their way here. Caleb returned the last call. Alana was petting Rex, telling him what a good job he'd done and checking him for injury. Fowler demanded a phone call and a lawyer.

Yoxall's voice was tense. "Caleb?"

"Yeah."

"Are you okay? There was this school shooting drill—"

"I know. I've got Fowler here, with a friend. They're restrained, but the friend has a broken arm. We may have found the evidence, but I'll leave it for you. When can someone get here?"

"I'm on my way. Had to call in some favors, but we can go wide now. Hang on, we'll be there soon."

He hung up, and Caleb returned the phone to his pocket.

"Alana." This was his chance to explain, before they got caught up in reports and statements.

Alana stood. "So, you're a cop?"

He nodded. "RCMP."

"And you've been undercover."

"Yes, I mean, not officially but—"

"You knew about me, before you got to Winnipeg. About my father, and my real name, the whole story?"

"Yeah. I did, but I need to explain—"

"Caleb, I'm not a genius, but I think I can connect the dots here. You were sent to find this evidence, right?"

"Not exactly. I was supposed to watch you, but it's not that straightforward."

"Maybe not. But this past week I've been robbed, almost abducted, driven halfway across the country and had my life threatened. I can't handle anything else right now."

His mouth opened, but then he closed it again. He wanted to justify himself, but that was selfish. If she needed time, he could give that to her.

"I'm sorry. You're right. Whatever you need."

"Should we finish digging up whatever you found?"

He glanced at the movie screen, empty squares amidst the grubby panels remaining, the fresh dirt piled underneath it. His arms ached just to consider using the shovel again. "No, I'll leave it in case it's evidence."

"Is it okay if I go over to that tree and sit in the shade with Rex?"

"You can do what you want to, Alana. You don't have to ask." Caleb had a gun trained on the two trussed bodies, just in case, but Alana didn't need to help him with that. His arm was bothering him, but he knew it was fine. He could take a little pain.

"But this is your case, right? And this is a crime

scene, or an attempted crime scene? I don't want to destroy evidence."

The words were good words, and she was right. It was best to leave the area undisturbed. But she was putting up barriers between them. Walls that meant they weren't friends, weren't maybe more than friends.

He hated it.

"Good work, Caleb."

"Thank you."

Yoxall watched the officers he'd been able to call in from the Toronto region process the scene. Caleb had been talking, for what felt like hours. First to officers who initially arrived, and then in more detail to Yoxall.

It was still daylight, but the shadows were growing long. "We're bringing in metal detectors. What you found was a piece of rusted pipe, but there might be something here. We've got enough on Fowler for now, but I'd like to get that evidence, if it exists."

Caleb was grateful for the words. He'd worked hard, and this had been difficult, but now a crooked cop was going to pay for what he'd done. Alana's father was still a fence but hadn't taken a life. There was a good chance Fowler's father would not be running for public office. The man might have had good ideas, but he'd demonstrated that he'd take shortcuts to get what he wanted, and those weren't the kind of people Caleb wanted running the country, or province, or even the police department.

"I'll put in a good word for you but I'm hearing rumors that you might be getting a call soon about the undercover work. You did well here. You were on your own, without resources, and still got your job done."

Caleb tried to smile. "I had help. I'm not sure what would have happened if Alana hadn't used the attack command for Rex. Fowler was ready to shoot someone. I think he was looking forward to it."

"Well, thanks to the three of you, he won't be shooting anyone. Not for a long time."

Caleb glanced around. The ruined drive-in was still busy. The ambulance had gone with Fowler's partner. Caleb's arm had been bandaged, but he wasn't seriously injured. Fowler was gone in another car, and the crime scene people were finishing up.

He didn't see Alana anywhere. Rex was being cared for by someone from a K-9 unit, but the woman he'd spent the last week with was gone.

"Where's Alana?"

"They've taken her in to make an official statement." When Caleb moved, Yoxall halted him. "You need to give your statements separately."

"I need to talk to her. Not about this, but—"

"Caleb." Yoxall's voice was kind, gentle. "Being undercover can be intense. Feelings can…stir up. But they're temporary. Alana is a nice woman, but she has a life to get back to, and so do you. I know your father is going to be proud of you. Don't make this into something it isn't."

Caleb's cheeks heated. Was that what this was? Just the effect of spending this time together, in an intense setting?

He wasn't sure he agreed with that. But maybe that was all it had been for Alana.

Chapter Twenty-Three

Alana leaned her head against the train window. She watched the trees rush by.

This train trip over the Great Lakes was a lot different than driving with Caleb and Rex. No one was following, there were no flat tires or overheated engines. No need to look up places to stay or check when the next gas station was available. She should be enjoying this. It was a beautiful excursion.

But her heart was hurting, and that was coloring everything. She'd thought there'd been something with Caleb. She'd been looking forward to returning home and getting to know him in ordinary life. But he'd been playing a role, and she hated that it made her feel stupid. Made her feelings seem childish. She hadn't been able to distinguish between a man befriending her for his job and someone who really cared for her.

And still she missed him. Missed him, even though she didn't even know if Caleb was his real name. If anything he'd told her was true. But then again, her mother had lied to her most of her life and Alana hadn't known. She wasn't sure what she could depend on as true right now.

Her mother had lied to her. Caleb had lied to her. Who else knew her story and her background and either actively lied or lied by omission? Was there anyone she could trust? She could trust God, at least, but even that… God had allowed this to happen. What else might He allow?

She was on a stage, playing a role, and she didn't know her lines. The play had changed. Did she want to stay in Winnipeg? Continue her practice? Live in the same house now that she knew what she did about herself? Should she go back to the name she'd been born with, and the city she'd grown up in for the first four years of her life?

Help me, Lord. I don't know even who I am, let alone what I should do.

"Good morning, Mr. Conners."

Alana wasn't surprised that he'd come to see her as soon as she was home. She stood in the doorway of her house, not sure she wanted to invite him in.

"Good morning, Alana. Is everything okay?"

"Did you not get a full report?"

It hadn't been difficult to figure out that Mr. Conners, who'd recommended his friend's son as a tenant for the garage apartment, knew everything that was going on. Caleb wasn't his friend's son, so that had been another lie. Did Mr. Conners even like her, or had keeping close to her mother and her been part of his job as well?

"I understand that you're upset, but I hope you'll give me the opportunity to explain."

Alana wanted to say no. She was tired of people lying to her and didn't want to hear any more lies. That was why she'd left Toronto without speaking to Caleb again.

But Mr. Conners had been part of her life since she was a child. Probably since she and her mother came here. And even if he was another person who'd hidden the truth from her, maybe he could answer some questions about her mother, now that she knew what questions to ask.

"Sure." Her voice was flat, but she held open the door and led him to the kitchen. "Coffee?"

"That would be kind of you."

She heard Mr. Conners sit down as she busied herself with the coffee maker.

"I'm pleased to know that you're out of danger, and that we now know the real story of what happened with your father. Your mother always worried about that."

Alana turned around. "How did you know all this? Why did Mom talk to you but not me?"

"I was in charge of your WitPro. After your father died, we didn't think there was much risk, so when I retired, no one else was assigned to you."

Alana gripped the countertop. "Why did she never tell me? I understand, when I was a kid, and I may have put us in danger unthinkingly, but as an adult, why couldn't I be told?"

Mr. Conners sighed. The coffee maker beeped, so Alana set a cup of coffee down in front of him, and some milk and sugar.

"I asked her, several times, if she'd told you yet. I thought you should know. She always told me she'd do it when the time was right, and that it was her decision. She made me promise to leave it to her."

Alana brought her own mug of coffee to the table.

"I don't know for certain, but I think she was concerned about how it might affect you, to find out the truth about your father. Her own feelings about him were conflicted. She worried about how you'd think of her, since she'd been married to him, and known what he was doing. And that she'd testified against him. She did that for you."

"For me?"

"Fowler had threatened you and your mother. It's why your father wouldn't testify on his own behalf. Your mother wanted witness protection for the two of you, but she had to offer something in return. And she insisted that it be through the RCMP, not the OPP, since that was the agency Fowler's father was part of, or the city police, since Fowler was a city cop.

"No one knew what Fowler Senior would do if his son's misdeeds came out. If he'd stand back and let justice be served, or if he'd interfere. He'd risen quickly in the OPP and there were suggestions that he might have taken shortcuts. Since Fowler Junior had an alibi, though fake, there wasn't enough evidence to convict him. We weren't sure how far his connections with the city police would go."

Alana twisted her mug around, watching the swirls of milk moving with the motion.

"Mom always seemed so brave. But you think she was afraid I'd judge her?"

"She gave up everything to keep the two of you safe, and you two were close. I think that if you had lost respect for her, she'd have found it very difficult."

Alana sighed. It was probably as close to an answer as she would get.

"It's hard to come to terms with this, that Mom lied all these years. And that you knew… Why didn't you tell me after she died?"

Mr. Conners leaned back in his chair. "I didn't know that she hadn't told you, not for sure. You might have decided you didn't want to talk about it. I considered asking you, but I had no idea how to pose a question that wouldn't tip you off if you didn't know. I wasn't sure how it would affect you, or even if it was necessary for you to know. You have a good life—did it need to be upset?

"Maybe the truth is that I was a bit of a coward as well. I didn't want to face your questions, and maybe accusations. Maybe your mother was right, that you were better off not knowing."

Alana was tense with frustration. "I'm not a child!"

"I know, but I'm not that brave. When you had the two break-ins, I spoke to someone I trusted. Someone who'd been part of settling your mother and you here. He was concerned and told me he was sending someone. Caleb Johnson. I don't know his real name, but he did a good job. You're here, safe, and there's nothing to threaten you."

Alana rubbed her face. "I feel so stupid. I thought there was something real between Caleb and me. It hadn't been even a couple of weeks, but we went through a lot together. It meant something to me, and it was just a job for him."

Conners reached over and held her hand. "Alana, you are a lovely and smart and good woman. The fact that this was his job doesn't mean he didn't have true feelings. I don't know about that. I'm sorry if you were misled by the circumstances, but you did nothing wrong. Did he cross any lines? Make you promises?"

Alana shook her head. "No. Nothing spoken. It was just…the way he looked, the way he acted—I thought something was there. But he was lying to me, too."

"I'm sorry, Alana. I'm sorry your heart was bruised. But I am grateful that he and the dog protected you. And helped you find the truth. We've prayed for you, and for him. That God would protect and guide you. And He will."

"Dad, can I talk to you for a minute?"

"Sure, son. Just to reiterate, you did good work. I'm proud of you."

"Thanks." Praise from his father still made Caleb feel good. He knew his father was pleased that Caleb was fulfilling the dream he himself hadn't been able to.

They settled in comfortable chairs on the deck of his parents' house. The sun was setting, and the air beginning to cool after a warm day.

"So, what's up, son?"

Caleb drew a breath. "I'm confused about something. This was my first shot at undercover, and it wasn't what I'd expected."

His dad nodded. "Probably feels that way for everyone when they first start."

"I understand that. But I'd thought I'd be among people who were breaking the law. And misleading and lying to them wouldn't bother me."

His dad raised his brows. "The lying got to you, eh?"

"It felt wrong. Especially when I was lying to Alana."

"We've brought you up to be truthful. I can't say I'm upset that lying isn't easy for you, but if you want to do undercover work, it's going to be your life."

Caleb rubbed a hand through his hair. "Does it get

easier? And if it does, is it going to creep back into my real life? Am I going to lie just to make my life easier?"

There was a pause, and Caleb knew his father was thinking through his answer. "I would hope not, Caleb, but I've never done undercover. It wasn't an issue for your grandfather, as far as I know, but we never discussed it before he passed."

Maybe Caleb needed to talk to someone who had dealt with these issues.

"And the other thing is Alana."

"The young woman you were protecting."

Caleb nodded. "We spent a lot of time together, during some intense events. I felt like we had a connection."

Caleb could feel his father's scrutiny. "What kind of connection?"

"Emotional. Romantic. I felt close to her and wanted to get closer still."

His dad grunted. "Interesting. What is she like?"

Caleb looked over the lawn. "She's brave and compassionate. Things get to her—she went through a lot while we were together—and she didn't pretend it was easier than it was, but she kept going. Stayed focused on what was the right thing to do, and did it even when she was scared."

"Attractive?"

Caleb's cheeks heated. "I thought she was beautiful."

His father nodded. "Do you love her? Is that what you're telling me?"

"Maybe? But Yoxall said that things like this happen in undercover. It's intense and feelings are inflated by that. They aren't real."

His dad studied him. "You're not sure if what you feel for this woman is real?"

"Exactly. I think it is. And that she felt the same. I didn't say anything—I couldn't, since I was lying to her the whole time, but there was something…"

His father cleared his throat. "Is she a woman you'd introduce to us?"

Caleb couldn't hold in a smile. "In a heartbeat. You'd love her."

His father smiled back. "I don't think people get that kind of attached undercover. It passes when the job does. Your grandfather had a lot of stories, and friends he worked with, and no one married someone they met while working."

"I wondered. The feeling isn't going away."

"Then maybe you need to talk to her."

Caleb leaned back in his chair. "She's gone back to Winnipeg. She didn't want to speak to me, once she found out I was a cop and I'd been lying to her."

His father put a hand on Caleb's arm. "It's your call, son. If you don't go talk to her, then she'll know it was just a job for you. If you think this could be more, you're going to have to go to her and talk about it."

"I don't know if she'll even speak to me."

"One way to find out. If she's not worth taking that risk for, then she's not the one you think she is."

Caleb sighed and nodded.

He'd prayed about this and done his best to work things out from his end. But he couldn't stop thinking about Alana. He wanted to talk to her throughout the day. He wanted to know how she was doing. He wanted to show her the photos he'd taken of her family's letters. He wanted to tell her everything he could about her father and what had happened. He wanted her to meet his family.

He didn't know if a person could fall in love after what they'd been through, but he suspected he had. She couldn't have done the same: he'd been lying the whole time. But maybe she'd consider giving this thing between them a chance.

But...

"You know, Caleb. If you want to go undercover, you're going to be away in dangerous situations for lengthy periods of time. You need to be honest with her about that. It's not much of a life for the person left behind."

That was the other thing that had him tossing in his bed at night. "Yeah. I can't imagine any person signing up for that, and I can't see myself asking that of someone."

"That's the crux here, isn't it?"

"What do you mean?"

"Caleb, I was proud when you said you wanted to work undercover. I admired and respected my dad for the work he did as an undercover cop, and I wanted to follow in his steps. Since I couldn't, it felt right that you would do it for me. But, son, that's not a burden I want to place on you. If that's not where you're being led, then don't do it to please me. I'm proud of you and the man you are, whether you're working undercover, doing other police work, or whatever way God leads you."

Caleb swallowed through the lump in his throat. "Thanks, Dad. I needed to hear that."

"Sounds like you have some big decisions ahead."

"I do."

Caleb sat in Yoxall's office, but this time he was the one who'd requested the meeting.

"So, what's up, Drekker?"

"I've been doing a lot of thinking. Talked to some guys and—"

Yoxall leaned back in his chair. "Had a taste of undercover, and not sure it's for you?"

Caleb jerked. "How did you know?"

"I've been watching you, Drekker. And you're not the first guy to rethink this."

"I feel as if I'd let people down if I backed out now."

Yoxall shook his head. "Better to know now. I wasn't sure you'd be able to handle this, which is why I haven't been rushing to get you into the program. Would you rather stay where you are?"

Caleb squared his shoulders. "Actually, I would like a transfer. Just not to undercover."

Chapter Twenty-Four

$\mathbf{A}$lana stroked a hand down the side of the cat on her examination table.

"She should be good now. Use the drops in her ears twice a day for a week. Let us know if there are any problems."

The elderly man on the opposite side of the exam table smiled at her. "Thank you. She keeps sneaking out of the house, and then we get things like this."

"Smokey was a stray, so that's the life she's used to, but she'll get more comfortable with you."

"Thank you, Doctor."

Alana watched her patient leave and let the smile drop from her face.

She'd immersed herself in her routine since she'd returned from Ontario. The first couple of nights in her house she'd been nervous, but her mind had finally embraced the knowledge that the person who'd been after her was no longer interested in her. Or free to pursue her if he were.

She'd need to testify if things went to trial, and that would mean a return to Ontario, but officers had been able to find the box her mother had buried. Not under the screen, where Alana had thought the movie indicated, but behind the concession stand. A place that probably meant something to her parents, but not something her mother had shared. They'd found the videotape and been able to restore it. Fowler had that serious crime to deal with. What happened with Alana and Caleb wasn't his priority now.

She tried to push thoughts of Caleb out of her mind. It was difficult. More difficult than it should be after the short time she'd known him.

The short time she *thought* she'd known him. She hadn't known the real man. She had to get over this, because she'd never see the man again unless they both had to testify. He'd moved on. She'd only been a job for him.

Her assistant knocked on the door.

"Can you fit in one more patient? Nothing serious, just a quick examination. It's a new patient—a Mr. Drekker."

Alana forced a smile. "Sure."

She didn't want to go home. The place was even more lonely now than it had been after her mother died. She wasn't sleeping well, and she was frustrated that she couldn't push thoughts of Caleb aside.

She forced a smile on her face again and opened the door to the other examination room.

She froze in the doorway.

"Caleb?" Then, as she looked beside him, "Rex?"

Rex came to her, pushing his head against her hand.

Caleb offered a small smile.

"Rex and I just drove back from Ontario."

Alana moved into the room. "Of course. You need to get your stuff."

Caleb shifted on his feet.

"Rex's handler had a serious heart attack, so I'm taking care of him for a while, since he's used to me. I'd like you to check him over—make sure he's okay after everything that happened."

With me, Alana thought, but didn't say that. "Of course. I'd be happy to. Give me a moment to lower the table so he can get on."

Rex hopped on without any fuss. All his vitals were normal. Alana kept her focus on the dog, doing her best to ignore the man in the room with her.

"He's good. With any luck that graze won't even scar."

"Thank you, Alana."

She lowered the table for Rex to get off.

"So, you still have your key, right? Once you have your things, you can drop it in the mailbox." She'd find somewhere else to be until they were gone.

Caleb ran a hand through his hair. "About that."

Alana stiffened.

"Do you have another tenant lined up?"

She shook her head. She'd been ignoring anything to do with the apartment.

"Would it be possible to extend my rental? Say for a year or so?"

Alana turned to the computer in the room, entering Rex's information, hiding her face from Caleb. Her hands shook as she typed. She swallowed and fought to keep her voice level.

"Why would you want to do that?"

"Turns out undercover work isn't for me."

Her fingers stilled. "It's not?"

"This case, with you, was the first and last time. I just can't handle the lying."

Oh. What had she thought he meant? At least she hadn't been wrong about him. He did have morals and ethics.

"Oh. But don't you have your regular job to do, back in Toronto?"

"I've asked for a transfer."

She turned to face him. Time seemed to stand still. Why did he need a rental here? "To Winnipeg?"

He nodded. "We did a good job with Fowler, so they're going to expedite the transfer. I've requested to join the K-9 unit here. There's a waiting list, and the training for the program is in Alberta, but I'm willing to wait and put in the work."

"What?" Alana's mind was having a difficult time grasping what he was saying.

"Turns out I like working with dogs. And I like Winnipeg."

She watched him closely, unsure if he was being truthful. "It gets cold in the winter. You haven't been through that yet. And windy. The days are short."

Caleb hunched a shoulder. "I'll adapt. Other people do. And I have good reason to be here."

"What?" Same question as before, but the request was different this time.

"Turns out I've fallen for someone who lives here, so if I'm going to have a chance for her to consider dating me, this is where I need to be."

He couldn't be talking about her, could he? But who else...

"Caleb, you can't be serious. You can't just move here, because maybe..."

"You know why I wanted to work undercover?"

The change in conversational direction threw her.

Alana didn't understand why he was asking her that. "No, how could I?"

"A big part of it was to make my dad happy, but we've worked that out. Another reason I thought that was my calling was because I haven't been able to find my special person. Maybe she didn't exist, and I could do valuable work while I was single, since undercover doesn't work well for people in relationships. But now I've found someone I want to be with. Forever. I want family and home, so undercover work is out."

"I don't know what to say." Everything she thought was up had been turned upside down.

Caleb moved to her, took one of her hands in his. "Tell me you'll give me a chance to make this up to you. I didn't pretend how I felt about you, and I want the chance to prove that.

"Just a chance. I won't stalk you, or be a nuisance, but I want a real chance. I've already had the transfer put in—I'm that serious. Tell me I didn't imagine that there was a connection between us."

Alana looked at her hand, wrapped in his, and then up to his face. She wanted this. She didn't know how or why her feelings had attached to him so strongly, but they had. She bit her lip. "Well, I do still need a tenant."

Caleb's smile almost split his face. "You won't regret it. I promise."

"When do you want to move in? For real?"

His eyes were focused on her face. "I was hoping to stay at the apartment tonight."

"Interested in dinner?" Alana's smile was shy.

"Anytime. Always."

She looked up, searching his face for the truth.

"I'll spend the rest of my life proving to you that I'm

not lying anymore. It's too soon to tell you, but I'm sure I'm in love with you. I'm just going to wait for you to catch up. As long as it takes—unless you ask me to go."

Alana put a hand on his face, the warmth of his skin heating the cold places inside where she'd been so hurt.

"You don't have to wait."

His eyes blazed, and his hand covered hers. "Really? Can you forgive me? I hated every time I couldn't tell you the truth. I promise it was only for the job."

"I can forgive you—I know you had a good reason. But never again, Caleb."

"Never. I promise."

He sealed his vow with a kiss, gentle and sweet, until Rex bumped into them and brought them back to the here and now. They laughed.

"Sorry, Rex. Caleb, if you're joining the K-9 unit, your next dog better get used to this."

Caleb smiled into her loving expression. "I'll request special training."

* * * * *